A Tigress Publishing Book

ISBN: 978-1-59404-028-3
1-59404-028-1
Library of Congress Control Number: 2010930331
Printed in the United States of America

Book Design : Steve Montiglio
Editor: Amelia Boldaji

10 9 8 7 6 5 4 3 2 1

Requests for such permission should be submitted to:
Tigress Publishing
4742 42nd Avenue SW, Box # 551
Seattle, Washington 98116-4553

I wish to dedicate this book to my parents and grandparents who saw their dreams crushed by the sudden turn of events. They kept the flame of hope alive in themselves and gave me the passion for finding freedom again.

Introduction

There is a fine line between reality and fiction. After all, who can say with certainty that his or her perception of reality is not laced with fantasy? Still, words have the power to create a different reality. Expressed in words, this new reality becomes a new world we can believe in. And it's good to remember things, how they were and how they could have been. We own that power, even in times when the reality of our circumstances suggests something different.

The book is based on a true story, however certain situations and details have been altered for dramatic purposes, and all the names of the people involved have been changed. This book represents many human beings who lived through the era of the Cold War. The times were rough, but beauty could still be found in the hopefulness of youth with its dreams, plans, desires, and love. No one has the power to reverse the flow of time, so the sacred events from our past cannot be returned, only remembered and embraced.

Part One
Slovakia
1966-1978

1

*M*orning came, and the boy did not notice. He was sleeping in an oversized bed covered with down comforters that looked like a white mountain compressing his seven year old body against the mattress. The bed was French; the bedroom was part of Uncle Feri's castle. The boy slept well, partly because the air was fresh, delivering a scent of the forest that was out behind the castle's wrought iron fence. The village was up, all the roosters had sung their songs, and only the bells hadn't chimed yet. That was supposed to happen any minute. Every Sunday the Catholic Church bells competed with the Lutheran Church bells, splitting the crowd of villagers into almost two equal parts.

It was the middle of July and the sun shone with all its strength. The temperature inside the room rose enough to make the boy sweat. First he kicked the comforters off, then he changed his position as if in a slow swing dance. The bells rang. He was up.

First the boy needed to figure out where he was. His parents often sent him to visit various places during the summer, so he was a bit confused when he woke up. There were the high ceilings, heavy draperies, and the four post bed as clues, but his grandparents owned a similar castle too. In the end it was the painting that gave it away. The painting was of a blue horse on a pink meadow, running towards a turquoise forest. It was an original work by Csontvary Kostka Tivadar, a Hungarian impressionist. The boy knew then that he was in his uncle's hunting castle in the country. It was late and he had missed church. He peeked out the small window beside him that revealed a winding road lined with chestnut trees and grassy ditches. A few people dressed in fancy black clothes were running towards the church. The boy realized that he was alone. He grabbed his shorts and slipped them on, then he buttoned up a cotton shirt. He was ready.

The brass door handle was high, so the boy used his weight to pull it down. The door opened without a sound. Uncle Feri oiled the hinges two times a year. It made him feel he was in charge, even though it was Auntie who wore the pants. The floor was covered with silk Persian runners and they tickled the boy's feet. The warm carpet stopped at the marble stairs so his feet had to adjust again to the cold stone. Down in the kitchen the boy found fresh bread, milk, butter, honey and chocolate powder. He wasn't very interested in eating, but he knew there would be no time for such boring needs later. He drank five big gulps of milk from a chipped mug, chased them with a rough bite of bread, then finished the milk.

The boy's mind was already wandering. An avid reader of Karl May's novels, he liked to imitate stories of the Wild West. He retrieved his weapons in the mud room: a birch bow and a few arrows, a wooden rifle covered with nails, a knife that wouldn't kill a teddy bear, and a toy hand grenade. He was a seasoned Indian warrior and there were enemies out there in the forest. The boy slipped out onto the back porch, across the lawn, and through the iron gate. The forest was his.

The forest also belonged to his uncle, Feri Keviczky, and the small castle was the only one left of three that had previously been owned by the Keviczky family. But that was of no interest to the boy. His name was Adam Keller, the nephew of Feri, Count Keviczky.

~

Madeleine was not happy. After 1949 everything seemed to have changed. The new Communist regime in Czechoslovakia was not in favor of the higher class. Industrialists and aristocrats were persecuted as the enemies of the state. As the daughter of a Countess, Madeleine was now doomed to limited opportunities and low paying jobs. Regardless of her higher education, knowledge of languages, and enormous love of literature, she was restricted to teaching at an elementary school level. It was only the newest government rule to prevent people like her from influencing a generation of students—fearing that she would transfer her aristocratic ideas into their little spongy brains. The official ideology was now linked to the Communist party and the glorious times of her parents were gone for good.

It was not supposed to have been that way. Madeleine had grown up in the sheltered world her father created for his four daughters. Madeleine played the piano and all four girls wore nice dresses made by the best tailors in Budapest. Most of the family trips were to Budapest or Lake Balaton. Madeleine and her family spent most of their time in the region's capitol and two months of the summer at the hunting castle in the mountains. The family owned acres of vineyards and orchards, a forest, and two other homes, one in the mountains and the other on Lake Balaton.

The entire family spoke Hungarian, German, and Slovak fluently. That was very common in the Austro-Hungarian Monarchy, and her father passed it on the girls. Their mother's name was Maria Agnes, but most people called her Agi. Countess Agi Keviczky. That's how it was before. Agi was a true countess, and a thinker. She spoke from a space of intellect, culture, and knowledge. She was all class and charm. Her husband, Attila, loved her so much that their romantic marriage was part of the social gossip in the region. Attila and Agi met at the school where they both worked. He was a young teacher and she was employed in the administrative office. They looked at each other whenever they believed no one was watching. He brought her flowers and asked her to come to a meeting of the Christian youth group. She came. They fell in love, and stayed in love with each other for more than a half century. Their first daughter was Madeleine. Madeleine's first son was Adam, who was, for the moment, the only Indian chief in the family.

The sounds of the forest were truly special and Adam

was respectful of nature. He was excited to be out there in the wilderness, hunting bison in his imagination. His bare feet found soft grass and he walked lightly through the trees. He could hear birds and wind through the large arbors, the grandfathers of the forest. After an hour of walking, Adam came upon a large meadow covered with cattle. His imagination transcended the Atlantic Ocean, and transformed the European cows into bison. Now was the time. He felt the obligation to feed the tribe. He slipped his bow from his shoulder and reached for an arrow. The arrow found its way to the string. Adam pulled the string all the way...

"What do you think you're doing?" a high pitched voice shouted. The hunt was over. A skinny girl with red hair stood nearby, looking at him angrily. Her hair was fluffy like cotton candy.

After trying to explain his game to the Hungarian farmer's daughter, Adam turned back to the castle. It was at the same moment that his Uncle Feri stepped outside the castle with his Havana cigar, asking his wife Margareta what was wrong with that nephew of theirs. How long can one boy sleep? Uncle Feri wondered.

Adam thought he knew his way home, but he got lost. After two hours of walking, worried and sweaty, he finally emerged from the forest. In front of him was a local reservoir for carp and pike. He knew his way from here, although it was another hour to the castle. He took off his shirt and slowly dipped his ankles in the water. As the water rose to his buttocks, it felt very cold. The water in the dam was always cold because the current brought the cool stream from the deep.

Swimming was pleasant, and Adam washed away the sweat from running in the forest. He had to go home now. Auntie Margareta had an issue about coming late for lunch. Sunday lunches were a sacred thing in Slovakia. Families gathered after church and shared news while feasting on chicken soup, deep fried Vienna schnitzels, potatoes, salad, dessert, and coffee from Vienna that was rare and inspiring.

And even if Adam had not been playing in his fantasy world, he would not have known what was happening at Uncle Feri's castle. He did not see the official Communist party vehicle parked in front of the renaissance structure. He did not hear the barking voices of the comrade commissars ordering Uncle Feri and Margareta to pack their few things and prepare to leave their home. Adam did not see Uncle Feri's angry face as he tried to tell the intruders to leave. Unfortunately, the tip of the Kalashnikov machine gun was too cold to negotiate.

"Feri, don't argue, we have to do what they say," Margareta whispered. The thugs kept barking instructions they were told to deliver. They gave the Keviczkys one hour to leave, taking only what they could carry. While the four armed men went for a smoke outside, Feri and Margareta had to act fast. Feri's face was red from high blood pressure as he brought their dusty suitcases from the attic.

Feri had lost his other, larger real estate holdings to the new regime a few years ago. They were living in the last home that seemed far enough away not to bother the Communist authorities. The Keviczky family had owned the small castle for several centuries and the rooms were filled with antique furniture from the time of the monarchy. French and Italian, Hungarian and Russian. Cupboards hid collections of china and silverware, and hundreds of little objects hand-picked by Feri all around Europe. Shelves in the living room were loaded with Meisen porcelain like frozen actors holding their expressions for all eternity.

Adam came in through the back door and caught Margareta's attention. "Jesus Adam, go get dressed, we have to go," she said franticly. Uncle Feri took a kitchen knife and started cutting paintings out of their frames. He had traveled around Budapest, Pressburg, Szeged, Vienna, and Prague buying paintings, often guided only by his impulsive love of art. Now he had to decide what was worth the risk of keeping, and what had to stay behind. The sharp knife slid between the edge of the paintings and the gold leafed frames. The boy never forgot the sound of the ripping canvas.

Like all children who are afraid, Adam cried for his mother. He followed Uncle Feri and his wife Margareta as they pushed their bicycles down the road, knowing that the village was watching from behind their curtains. The backpack was heavy for Margareta, who was a woman of science and had a doctorate from the Charles University in Prague. Now she carried only the few possessions she had left in a backpack and two suitcases. The suitcases hung from the handlebars of her old bicycle.

Uncle Feri pushed a second bicycle loaded with suitcases, wicker baskets, and a bottle with water.

Adam was crying, and he refused to carry anything. They walked several kilometers to a train station. There Adam could smell the urine from the men's bathroom, roasting klobasa at the concession stand, and the beer at the open air pub. The trains smelled of coal and steam and Margareta felt the weight of everyone staring. Many knew Count Feri and his wife, and she was very afraid. She expected a car to screech down the dusty road, men jumping out with bad intentions. Time felt like tar flowing slowly and painfully, but after two hours the train finally arrived. The three of them pushed their way into the sweaty railroad car, abandoning the bicycles at the train station. The trip was like a silent exercise in lip reading. Uncle Feri and Margareta whispered, sometimes nodding towards the boy. His parents' names came up occasionally, and all Adam hoped was that he would see his mother soon.

⁓

Madeleine first heard the bad news through a terrible connection over the phone. She was living in the capital with Adam's father Samuel and his entire family. Feri called through an operator from the local post office. It was all terrible, frightening news. Madeleine left at once. She had to see her son.

The six hour long trip by train to pick up Adam felt like an eternity. Madeleine's mind raced, bringing up memories of when her parents lost the family estate. Her parents used to live in their town villa in the Hungarian speaking south until they received a document from the people's government about confiscating their villa and their hunting lodge. That had happened in 1950, and the family continued to keep a low profile because they still owned another villa that was tucked in a remote part of the provincial capital. No trace was ever left and no receipts were kept of the items already confiscated by the government. Now the same thing had happened to Uncle Feri. Madeleine knew that it was best not to resist and save their lives. Thousands had already vanished in Russia since the initial seeds of communism in 1917. At least they still had a life there, although Madeleine knew not to mention her aristocratic background to anyone outside the family.

Madeleine spent two days with Uncle Feri and Margareta. Stories were told and damages were assessed. Life had to go on. It was better to live in Bratislava, Madeleine told Uncle Feri, in a large city with thousands of nameless people. Her husband Samuel was not an ideal man but he had a special sense of family adherence. Madeleine was thinking of their family as she held Adam in her arms and he slept to the rhythmic sound of the wheels hitting the joints of the railroad tracks. The train was hot and smelled of sweat and food, but Madeleine didn't notice any of it. She was holding her son and dreaming about his future.

A true beauty on the Danube River, Bratislava was neither big, nor small. It was just right. The downtown historic core was almost a millennium old. Most buildings still looked good, though their destiny was not so bright. The new era of socialism would bring ignorance and a lack of common sense for maintenance, so deterioration was inevitable.

Yet the beauty was inherent in the stones, bricks, columns and sculptures that were organized in a perfect, yet seemingly arbitrary order. Winding narrow streets meandered uphill to the old castle. Bratislava was once an important city. Called Pressburg in German, and Poszon by Hungarians, it was a coronation town for the Austro-Hungarian Monarchy. Thousands of small shops and cafes made up the historic center of the city. In any pastry shop, you could choose from dozens of different kinds of sweet indulgences.

The city had seen things beyond any one man's comprehension. Emperors, empresses, princes, and industrialists, as well as writers, musicians, and bohemians had all walked the city streets. The gossip and the romance of the different times was as constant as the branches of the chestnut trees that lined the banks of the river Danube. On Sundays, honorable people promenaded along the street-front cafes, greeting friends with a tip of their hats.

All this beauty was just pollution in the eyes of the new administrators who destroyed synagogues, churches, and palaces to make room for intimidating concrete monsters symbolizing the new rule. As the Communist government gave orders to demolish the very heart of the old town, a wedge of concrete was driven between the historic center and the castle hill. Ironically, they called it the New Bridge and it caused more problems than it solved.

Adam did not understand any of this yet. He was still a child. He was still able to observe the world playfully, almost as a surreal work of literature.

Adam could not remember who he was in previous lives, and yet he believed in the strange possibility of coming and leaving, reappearing under different circumstances, sometimes for better and other times for worse. At times he felt a sense of purpose and serendipity that was never totally serendipitous. His physical life had started with an unexpected power outage caused by a big summer storm. The hospital was working by candlelight. Right after he passed through the entry gate of this world, the power came back on, making his mother think he was somehow linked to bringing light, as if he were a new Prometheus.

His mother often told him this story, and she explained that it was the circumstances of his birth that made him instantly independent, released to roam freely for his entire life. He was a child needing no supervision. Neither of his parents ever checked his homework, and they were pleasantly surprised when Adam graduated from the university with honors. Adam often felt as if everything he was supposed to learn came from suspicious sources, chancy happenings, and twists of fate. He got used to hard work, but he also learned that in tough situations something would eventually happen to turn the tide around.

As an example of this, Adam's best friend Igor was enrolled in the only school that offered English language classes, but Adam was not registered anywhere. On the day of the entry tests, the two boys went to school together, pretending that Adam belonged. The exams took forever, and because Adam was not on the list, he and Igor found themselves alone on the bench in the hallway. All the children were gone and the teachers were about to lock up the classroom. Adam played naïve and insisted that he was invited too. Though they couldn't find his file anywhere, the committee took him in and his results were among the best of all the applicants. After a small bribe, both Igor and Adam got into the school and started to study English.

⌐⁓⌐

"How do you do, Mr. Smith?" the teacher called to one of the students.

"I'm quite all right," the student responded.

For both Igor and Adam, English was love at the first sight and it stayed a passion of theirs for the rest of their lives. By the time they were fifteen, they both spoke it fluently. Adam used his new language skills to engage tourists in conversations about the countries they were from, obtaining books of English and American literature, and for trading Czechoslovakian money for the hard currency he needed for special treats. Perhaps an access to the spoken word in different languages— Adam avoided the word *foreign*, as it indicated something alien—gave him a new taste of freedom. It was freedom of communication and it registered as an entry on Adam's long list of desired freedoms.

Adam was also obsessive about reading. He read all he could get his hands on. The classics and the moderns. Dostoevsky, Tolstoy, Hemingway, Kerouac, Stendhal, the Scandinavians, the Russians, the Americans, the British. He read late into the night, consuming pages like some paper eating monster. The library system was selective about their readers and the Communists had created a strict system of control over who could borrow which book. There were also restrictions in place for banned books. Libraries rated individual's party adherence in order to determine how much access they were given. Adam's library rights were low, yet he managed to borrow his friends' IDs for getting to the good stuff.

The parody of forbidden fruit. Solzenicin, Milan Kundera, George Orwell; they were the best stuff. Even books about Gandhi were hard to get. The idea of passive resistance was a threat to the insecure nature of the totalitarian regime. The official ideology already seemed purely utopian to Adam, in spite of his young age. Any half intelligent person could see the lies and pretension of a corrupted regime. Family conversations spun around a very clear and present danger of persecution against many relatives. Adam grew very old for his age.

Adam had many friends however. One special group of friends was the sons of blue collar workers from the chemical plant. They were smart boys, not too shy, and their collective hobby was firearms. After the war many attic spaces were a cache of German rifles and pistols. Collecting fine pieces of steel with historic value became a passion and obsession for many people. The boys particularly liked the Mauser rifles, since these were very powerful. Adam often joined the group on their trips to the adjacent forest, just past the airport runways. The rifles were an escape from the land of rules—something thrilling and dangerous. Some of the ammunition was the so called dum-dum, a core of steel wrapped in lead and cased in brass with a concave tip. The shell was full of strong gun powder and Adam was the group's designated sharp shooter.

Another fun activity was fishing with hand grenades in the winter. The boys pulled the pins, and threw the grenades into the pond near the Bulgarian farm. The detonation stunned the carps and the boys pushed the fish to the shore with long poles. The wind blew fresh powder snow across the fields. The boys returned home red cheeked, bringing with them the trophy fish for dinner.

Some winters were awfully cold around Bratislava. Everything was frozen and trips to the nearby forests were quite challenging. Crossing frozen creeks and icy railway bridges was treacherous. But the boys were pragmatic and resourceful. They were never caught by surprise, and they were also sensitive to the spirit of the times. They sensed when the money around the households was sparse and meat was not on the menu, and they resorted to hunting. This time it wasn't just a boy's imagination as Adam joined his friends at midnight to venture out in the moonlit forest.

The boys outfitted their rifles with flashlights and invented clever camouflages for the weapons, often pretending they were fishing poles wrapped in blankets. It was unlikely to meet too many people on the streets at night, but they took precautions just in case. Once they were at the edge of the city they could unwrap the rifles and proceed without so much theater. The forest was bright as moonlight reflected off the fresh snow. Most trees around the area were bare in the winter. The only visible dense spots in the trees were often mistletoe or pheasants. When the forest devoured the group of small figures, their senses were heightened. They were still not far from villages and the airport. There were solitary houses and occasional cops driving on the country roads. A shot from a large caliber rifle was certainly heard from miles and miles away.

Adam was one of the two designated shooters since he had a gift of being able to see in dim light. Others kept lookout for bundles in the branches. As they got deeper into the forest, a few of these bundles showed against the moonlit night sky. Adam aimed in their direction, turned on the flashlight, and adjusted the aim. Bang! They got five or six pheasants in no time. At night, once one bird was shot, the others stayed put because they could not see to fly away. Now the young hunters had to run fast in case the local police station was alerted to the piercing gunshots. The boys were in top shape and their little hearts pounded from the excitement. The cops tried to block the dirt roads and their headlights pierced through the night. Strangely, the hunters became the hunted, but the boys managed to escape. They knew every twist of the road and every tree. They ran along the banks of the creek, crossing over a narrow railroad bridge, and they made it home before the break of dawn.

Looking back as a grown man, Adam did not

understand why it was all right with the parents of these working class boys to find the pheasants in the refrigerator. Maybe the means did not matter, the results were only consumed. Amen.

⁓

The sixties were great years for all free minded people in Czechoslovakia. Sometime around 1960, the failure of the Communist economic plans and the resulting recession opened up space for other ideas. Little by little, people were becoming aware of better ways to live, and the brain power of a highly capable nation was waking up from a bad dream. The Soviet propaganda was never fully accepted by the highly cultural Czechs and Slovaks who shared a rich history of democracy. Slowly, the lust for freedom made its way to the mainstream. By 1968, Czechoslovakia was breathing the air of new times. Something amazing and beautiful started to happen. Literature was fertile with excellence and art was exceptionally progressive. Slovak and Czech artists were exploring the liberty of a world without censorship. Milan Dobes made kinetic sculptures and installed them along the freeways in America. Light shows were popular. And people were smiling again. Happiness and the air of new times were factors that mattered.

People were ready for the true and honest political leadership. That dream arrived in a person called Alexander Dubcek. Dubcek was elected as a secretary of the leading party by the people in free and democratic elections. Everyone sensed a process of liberation from the Soviet-imposed system. It was simply in the air. But towards the summer of 1968, dark clouds were amassing east of the joyful and carefree people of Czechoslovakia. On August twenty-first, Adam woke up to an unusual noise. It was the persistent dark noise of war machines. Quickly, he noticed the neighbors talking in the corridors of the building. Everyone left their doors open to communal discussions as if they needed some collective process to clarify their fears.

With the aid of other puppet Communist pets from other East European countries, the Soviet Army had rolled tanks and army trucks into Slovakia, advancing towards Prague. Adam dressed fast and hooked up with his buddies from the building. Outside, the lines for food were miles long as people anticipated times with no supplies and conflict. The boys ran to the arterial road where the main noise was coming from. The experience of standing ten feet away from a convoy of deadly military vehicles was thrilling and frightening. The noise was almost unbearable as the metal caterpillars demolished the road. They drove at top speed, spreading diesel fumes along the boulevard.

Adam and the boys were not alone. Hundreds of young men and women lined the road with curiosity in their eyes. They were surprised and afraid of the unknown. Adam and his friends came up with an idea. They gathered rocks and concrete blocks from the nearby construction site as if it was a new game. Then, with a daredevil thrill, they threw the pieces of concrete in the tanks' path, only to see them pulverized by the massive force. The tank commander stuck out his head and brandished a pistol, waving it at the boys.

Those were times of patriotism and times of betrayal. Adam learned much later that several brave men and women were killed during the early days of the invasion. The photograph of a man baring his chest just inches from a gaping barrel of a tank became an icon of the resistance. At the time though, the boys just ran for their lives. They began painting over street signs, writing "Ivan go Home" with red paint. Even though the boys were hardly aware of what it meant, the political leadership was quickly trapped and disabled. The free broadcasting ended with gunshots for background music. The script became chaotic, and actors were endangered. People had to keep their opinions well hidden from the ears of the KGB and the Secret Police. No one was free anymore. Neither the oppressed, nor the tyrants.

Of course, when people don't have a choice, they cannot enjoy their freedom. But surprisingly, the oppressors aren't free either. They are constantly afraid of vengeance by the innocent victims of their brutality. They are afraid of the higher power of the political ladder. They cannot sleep. One day, they will be punished. It's just a matter of time.

3

The circus came to town every spring. The wagons were hitched behind tractors and trucks, and the entire tent with its rings and benches was built fresh in each city. Adam was mesmerized by the whole scene as he and his friends watched the carnies erect the tent on a large vacant piece of land. Monkeys and tigers were caged separately behind strong metal bars, and the elephants were put to work in construction. Holes were dug for the long poles. Thick ropes tied to the poles helped the elephants erect the basic structure and cover it with the cloth. Men with huge muscles hammered metal pins into the ground to tie down the tent. Gypsy looking women walked around the men with the big muscles, and the skinny jugglers rehearsed their numbers in between the parked trailers. A mechanical calliope played colorful tones through the loudspeakers. Adam looked at the tunnels leading to the backstage where the tigers would be set free and the trainer would take over so the beasts wouldn't eat the audience. The curious thing close to a miracle, Adam thought, was that the tigers would not eat the horses while riding on their backs during the show.

Suddenly, a strange man—a mixture of a clown

and a magician—came over to the group of boys. He spoke the sounds *abracadabra* and pulled a dove from his sleeve. Then he showed the boys several tricks with coins and cards, and told the boys about the faraway places the circus had traveled. When he was finished he turned to Adam and said, "You will go to a faraway place where you will find treasure."

Adam kept the image of the magician in his mind all his life. During the two weeks while the circus was in town the boys hung around the fence and tried to peek in the tent because they had no money to go in and see the performance. They observed all the activity around the tent and backstage while the performers were getting ready instead. It was clear that the jugglers were related to the contortionists, and their children performed the high wire act. Adam saw that one monkey was totally domesticated and free, while all the others were kept on leashes or inside their cages. The tigers were huge, and during their performance all the circus people were on a high alert, nervous and yelling, much like an agitated hornets' nest. The elephants were tied to a thick iron rod driven into the ground by the muscle men, and they produced piles of dung and swayed from side to side. Occasionally, their penises would hang down almost to the ground, and the boys poked each other in disbelief. Although he didn't tell his friends, Adam was always searching in vain for another glimpse of the clown magician.

Back in the realism of the everyday city life, Adam was a part of an unofficial book club. The rules were simple. You could borrow a book from the pool and read it overnight. It was a precaution to keep the reading time short. If a book lingered in some person's hands longer, he was considered untrustworthy and his membership was terminated. Adam was a fast reader and he never broke the rules. Besides, the group was fascinating. Professors of philosophy, writers, poets, even children of high ranking Communists, met to drink beer and discuss books until the last streetcar moved through the old downtown. They gathered in private places, usually at one of the members' apartment. Adam gained a trove of knowledge from those intellectuals. He also learned social skills and the art of conversation, particularly respecting other people's ideas and opinions.

As much as he could, he filled his time studying languages, music, and foremost, art. Even his guitar teacher was Adam's fantasy lover for almost a year. A young blond with beautiful lips, she mesmerized Adam with her fingers as she demonstrated difficult parts of musical scores. Her lips were often wet from eating oranges, her favorite snack. Adam thought it was strange that she always managed to have oranges. Tropical fruit was hard to come by, but every day she peeled an orange while listening to her students play. Her sheer beauty and gentle attitude made her students fall in love with her along with the musical instruments and the music she sold.

Eventually, the lovely teacher got married and quit teaching at the music school. Adam kept playing guitar, though he did not stay at the music school much longer. He and his new friends at the high school formed a band and played forbidden music from the West like the Beatles, Pink Floyd, and Freddy Mercury. Of course, for an official performance they prepared Slovak and Czech rock music. They could play rock music from the other side of the tracks only at private gatherings.

Adam's grandfather also grafted the love of art on Adam's young mind. Together Adam and his grandfather spent many hours discussing Goya, El Greco, and Van Gogh, and by the time Adam turned fifteen he had been to some of the best museums of art in the communist part of the world. The museum in Budapest was one of them, and the art collection in the National Gallery was etched into Adam's memory. Grandfather Atilla Zaborsky always wanted Adam to study art, and so it was only natural that Adam enrolled in an evening school of Fine Art at the age of fifteen.

The building where Adam studied was a single story, stucco-covered warehouse, with tall windows and high ceilings. It smelled of turpentine, linseed oil, clay, and glue. The teachers were graduates from the Art Institute in Prague or Bratislava, and they brought their own talent to the teaching process. Some were also very talented musicians, like Gabi Stankova, who was well known for her folk ballads. To top this, they were a true bohemian group and they brought their love of life to the studios. They also liked to share. Baskets with fruit and other food were offered casually in the classroom. Music filled the atmosphere in the ateliers like a warm blanket of all things, and students remembered the teachers best for their kind smiles. It is amazing how inexpensive a smile is, and how much it gives the recipients.

At school Adam learned to draw still lives first, then figures. Live models came to the classrooms, and the teachers arranged their bodies in aesthetically pleasing poses while the students painted for hours. During bathroom breaks some students strummed their guitars, and others read from the stack of art magazines. Many future Slovak personalities were bred at the community art schools. None of this was possible however at the official state run Art Institute. There the Communist party kept their spies, and the teachers were selected by their willingness to teach propaganda.

The evening art school was unofficial enough to create trust and friendships. This opened Adam's world as nothing had before. Stevo Malinsky was one of Adam's closest friends there. He looked like George Harrison with long hair and a mustache. Ten years older than Adam, Stevo knew most of the famous personalities of the underground. He had his hands on stuff that blew Adam's mind, from all the music records of British and American rock bands to loads of art magazines and books by exiled authors. Everything came from Stevo's connections with the underground. Stevo created a truly special atelier for himself and those privileged friends of his. In the basement of the apartment building where he lived, Stevo discovered an unused crawl space under the stairs, full of construction debris from the time the building was constructed. The ceiling was fourteen feet tall, which allowed for a loft with a few futons, candle holders, and shelves for glasses and bottles. It was a true hippie's paradise and they nicknamed it "the cave".

Stevo's place became so popular, that a schedule had to be kept and people signed up for space to do band rehearsals there. Parties were held on Saturday evenings with guest speakers, musicians, and always, wine connoisseurs. For Stevo, freedom meant there were no rules and all fun. Stevo became a Slovak version of Egon Bondy, known in the underground for being a catalyst. Most importantly, Stevo taught the younger boys how to paint without self-censorship. He taught them how to be themselves at all times, and how to train themselves to disregard all imposed truths. Heavenly music played in the background as couples made out up on the loft, and other guests developed black and white photography or painted wild pictures. Adam was Stevo's right hand, bringing some of his own talent to the organization. In spite of the wild and crazy Czechoslovakian spirit, someone had to keep things running, organize cleaning duties, and update schedules.

"Adam, the cave is a mess. You know who is coming tonight? Jan Zeman," Stevo said excitedly over the phone.

"Are you serious? Is he bringing that singer, you know, that sexy brunette who sings with the band?" Adam asked.

"I'm sure. He's all over her. Hey, we need wine and beer, and some cheese. Can you get someone to clean up?"

"Consider it done. But I started a new painting there. It's still fresh and smells like turpentine," Adam said, worrying about damage. Last time he had a painting there some drunk idiot painted over his work.

"Bring it upstairs to my place, it will be safe," offered Stevo.

Adam and couple of regulars cleaned the bottles and dishes from the last party and borrowed a vacuum cleaner to run over the dust in the cave. By the time they were done people were starting to arrive. Stevo set up the amps and guitars as some guys started to play chords and melodies in a soft jazz-rock style, and other people arrived with food and beer.

"I love this monochromatic stuff," commented Jan on Klein's blue paintings. "The pigment just sits on the surface, as if nothing was holding it down. I feel like I can blow it off."

"Why do you think he uses blue?" asked Adam.

"Blue has always served as a color of the divine," Stevo said. "More importantly, Klein achieves to trigger meditation and captures the transcendental in our perception of life. It is about presence of the absent."

"I love the paintings with imprints of the female bodies. They leave their mark on the canvas as if they were just there, and you wonder if it is still warm. The paint that stays on their bodies makes them a work of art as well, don't you think?" Adam said thoughtfully.

"When art is all that you do, you may soon become an art object yourself. You are selling an illusion, much like Warhol," said Stevo. They were quite proud of Andy Warhol, because he was from the eastern part of Slovakia.

A month ago Adam and Stevo had orchestrated a big gathering on a meadow near Bratislava. Their friend Tomas was selected to represent a Communist. They dressed him in a red suit and placed a special harness under his coat. As if in a serious drama, they created a mock public trial, reading a list of "crimes" committed by the apparatchiks in the government. Then they proceeded with a punishment in front of a hundred or so spectators.

It was clear to most that this was a theater, however when the "Communist" was hanging from a limb of a big oak tree, some cops showed up. There was an instant clash as they tried to arrest a few people randomly. Stevo, Adam, and Jan had to cut Tomas from the tree and start running. It was chaos since half of the people didn't know what was really happening. In the end only the drunks in the crowd were arrested. They were thrown in jail for a few days for questioning, but they didn't know a thing. It was a great event, because the spectacle was very clear, the message was unambiguous, and it made people aware of the opposition within.

Ever since 1968, when the Russian tanks rolled through towns and villages all the way to Prague, freedom of speech no longer existed. Anyone who publicly expressed disagreement with the regime's ideology was arrested and persecuted. The crackdown on free thinking people by the puppets of the Soviet Empire brought fear and resignation to everyone.

The year 1977 brought the big opposition movement however. Most people secretly listened to Radio Free Europe and the Voice of America broadcasts. It was hard for the Communists in Czechoslovakia to keep people ignorant. In addition to the radio broadcasts there were also the Austrian and German television programs that exposed some of the official lies.

But the regime was still strong, threatening people with prisons, discrimination, and restrictions. All this resulted in a culture of escapism and people turned to drinking, and in some cases, slipped into depression and resignation. Other people were involved in secret dissident movements and opposition. These people were the spice of the nation.

Adam was on the side of the opposition, but he didn't think about it much. He certainly didn't think of himself as some kind of hero. He was used to keeping his mouth shut, except when he was certain who he was speaking with. This precaution worked for many years, but not everyone was so lucky.

By summer Adam had already transformed into a young artist. Of course he was still learning, but the fire of passion has been ignited. The awakening came all at once and on many levels. Adam was also growing into a handsome young man. His dark brown hair and equally dark, inquisitive eyes were gentle and deep. He kept a lot of secrets already. His entire life would be about keeping secrets. Communism was like that. Those who disagreed with the official ideology had to keep a low profile and hope that no one would turn them in. On the other hand, it was essential to keep the rebellion alive because the regime kept taking freedoms away.

Soon after World War II, the politicians divided the world in two blocks and built barbed wire fences between friends and families. Fences can be a very delicate phenomenon. Some people like to build them. They build them between their yards and properties. They build them to separate themselves from other people. Fences are built to protect the insiders from that which is outside—the danger of the unknown. Fences are also built to lock some people in, to restrict their freedom of exploration beyond those boundaries. Both are necessary sometimes.

For Adam, fences represented an obstacle, a barrier

to his chance to decide his own destiny. By the time he was thinking for himself, the entire country had become a big prison.

No one was allowed to travel freely unless it was to travel to neighboring countries with similar fences around them. Adam had seen Hungary, Poland, Rumania, Bulgaria, and East Germany, but he thought they were just a part of a bigger prison. With a standard passport, people took vacations and went on shopping sprees for unusual goods. Tasting the uncommon was a passion by itself. But only those privileged enough could travel beyond the barbed wire fences. Usually they were associated with some branch of the Communist party, or they belonged to a team representing the country in a storefront fashion, like sportsmen or ballet dancers. Others tried to bribe their way out.

Adam and his friends knew they had little chance of leaving. Instead, the boys often watched the fences and told each other stories. The fences at the border were complex. First, there was a chain link fence along the road to prevent people from getting close to the border. A few feet back there were multiple, tall chain link fences with barbed wire on top. The ground in between was plowed and raked so that any footprints were clearly visible. A watch tower was erected every three hundred yards apart. The patrol was equipped with machine guns and dogs that guarded their post day and night. The border near Bratislava was also delineated by the River Danube, thus making it even more difficult to get across.

The boys often speculated about people on the other side. How many cars did they have?

Did they have better houses? More toys? They knew

about some of the things, since the Austrian TV couldn't be blocked. Austria was politically neutral, at least in some ways. While the boys talked, Adam dreamed about going to Hawaii some day, seeing distant places and living in a place he felt was meaningful.

⌒

Being present where it mattered was a tempting subject. In Adam's dreams there were many scenarios for his future life and he and his friends often talked about their hopes, the joyful moments and the individual struggles. It appeared that on a basic, human level they were all the same and equal. The essential human condition required similar maintenance, regardless of the regime, time zone, weather, and wealth. Health and satisfaction were the obvious common denominators. But that was also the only similarity. Adam knew that people all over the world shared a love of literature, poetry, and music. What was dramatically different were the roads available to them in order to achieve their goals. While the Western system worked on one level, the workings of the Eastern system were trickier. First, there was the structure of the official government, based on a utopian idea of a society that operates as a family of altruistic individuals, happy to provide for others. Many brilliant minds subscribed to this ideology. Marx, Engels, Lenin, Trotsky and other brethren alike, all believed it was possible. Over the years, greed, anger, jealousy, and insecurity were added to the recipe. Then corruption, revenge, and lust. The real structure of communism was revealed after the proletariat leaders tasted power. Power tasted sweet and it certainly corrupted. Its smell reminded them of money, and of love for hire. Once they tasted that strength they became addicted. There were no treatment centers for this disease.

Adam did not comprehend the complexity of this artificial structure, nor did he know all the ingredients and dangers of the system. He was learning from his mentors little by little as he ran against invisible walls and glass ceilings. Every attempt to visit the West officially ended in the file cabinets of the government bureaucrats. Should anyone try to apply more than once they then became a subject of investigation by the secret police. Those who did travel had to be cleared first by the authorities, and half of them never came back. Defections were a way of escape from the black and white world to the Technicolor dream. The sacrifice was that they had to leave everything behind. Freedom is not only fragile, it is open to interpretation.

*I*n Bratislava, people enjoyed the last week of their summer vacations. Children ran around the public swimming pools playing ping-pong and tennis, and Adam was excited to be home. He was especially curious about the fact that the school where his mother taught had an official friendship with a school from East Germany. There happened to be a German class visiting Bratislava that summer, an exchange trip for students between twelve and seventeen years old. The blond, German-speaking children were enjoying a change of environment as much as the Slovak kids enjoyed having them stay.

"Ich heise Kirsten," a young girl said, introducing herself to Adam.

"Ich heise Adam, und Ich vohne in Bratislava. Bist Du aus Deutchland?" he asked, as if that was not obvious from the beginning. Sometimes he felt embarrassed by his own mistakes.

"Wir sind aus Warnemunde, bei Rostock." Her mouth was moving, and Adam became mesmerized. Her lips were full and defined, her hazel colored eyes soft, and her rich hair like the sunshine. She was a true German.

Before the end of that day, they fell in love. It was the first time for both of them. Kirsten was a year younger than Adam. She told him she had kissed boys in Germany, mostly to explore the techniques. Adam had not kissed any girls yet, he had only lived a boy's life with boy's games and he did not quite understand the science of romance. He had only discovered his sexuality a couple of years ago, when his friend Igor shared his father's smuggled Playboy magazines. Adam had also experienced the urges of his body while reading the erotic parts of classical literature from his parents' library. With Kirsten though, it was a new feeling. He was kissing a beautiful girl with lips made in heaven. Everything was colored with the hues of sunsets.

Their kisses were the extent of their exploration, but they sufficed, filling the cavities of their young hearts with warmth and devotion. They couldn't part, and later, when the summer was over, Adam wrote to Kirsten about his love. Life, school, art, and social time continued throughout the year as usual. Only the letters reminded them of the thrill of being in love.

Adam had progressed in art and music effortlessly. He handled school subjects without much trouble, and became very popular as a band member. The government was still telling people that capitalism was rotting and deteriorating, and it would soon be replaced by the power of the working class. Adam's friends knew the scent of that rot. To them, it smelled of perfume and freedom. The freedom to decide for yourself and be able to take your destiny in your own hands.

The Communist government created a special plan for each individual at the time of their birth, and decided what he or she would be allowed to achieve during their lifetime. Once they had decided, you were discouraged to study or do anything else. You could only pursue what someone else had prescribed for you. For each individual, that was the beginning and the conclusion of their possibilities. A few areas of life were controlled to even more extreme measures, such as the arts and the public education system. If you were not deemed safe for the regime, you were barred access to higher education unless you pursued a degree in engineering or agriculture. It was virtually impossible to study fine art, film, or drama without either having a Communist pedigree or bribing the official administration for admission.

Because he understood very well that artists could be dangerous, Adam quietly advanced in art, especially drawing and painting. His technique was good and his knowledge of philosophy and history gave him a broad context for inspiration. His work started to be known as progressive and daring. He was different, bringing fresh and new approaches to anything he started. The results may have been limited by his access to materials and technology, but nevertheless by the age of eighteen he had a handle on most fine art techniques, including sculpture. Many ideas and truths were revealed to him during his four years of work and friendship at the evening school of art.

The next summer, Adam signed up for a reciprocal camp in East Germany, on the coast of the Baltic Sea. The train journey was long, and he sat with the other students in cramped sleeper cars full of luggage and food. Most people carried a bag of food for the trip since it was not cheap to eat in the diner and the cars smelled of klobasa and Hungarian salami. When they arrived to Rostock before travelling to Warnemunde, Adam couldn't wait to see if Kirsten would be at the train station waiting with the other Germans. When he saw her they greeted formally in front of the chaperones, but Kirsten had a gift of talking without words. She smiled, expressing all her love through her eyes.

They all stayed at an official Youth Camp of the Freie Deutsche Jugend organization, but no one cared about the politics. The buildings were practically on the beach, just over the dunes from the sound of the waves that kept everyone awake for the first night. Besides being a port town, the area had a nice historic center. Small shops and café umbrellas lined the streets, offering refuge from the relentless sunshine.

Kirsten and Adam were carefree and happy. Holding hands, they walked miles of the sandy beach collecting rocks and tossing them in the cold waters of the Baltic. The water was always cold, regardless of the summer heat. The beach was furnished with huge wicker shelters that looked like small houses. The visitors turned the shelters downwind for protection from the wind and sand. Those who did not have a spare coin had to build a sand dune before stretching their blanket in the valley.

Adam felt a difference in the way he measured time and space. Being in love had carved each moment in his memory. After dinner, the young couple went out walking on the beach again. Kirsten's hands were wrapped around Adam's waist and shoulder, her head leaning against his arm.

"Do you miss home, Adam?" she asked, presuming he wouldn't. All their feelings seemed strangely identical those days.

"Nein," he replied, "I want to stay with you. A year is too long to wait."

They stopped, realizing they were alone far away from the camp. The sunset had turned into twilight and it was growing darker with every second. Kirsten kissed him, invading his mouth with her tongue. It felt like hundreds of little electric shocks. Their silhouettes became fused and she pulled him down onto the sand behind a dune. Adams lips delivered tiny kisses down the buttons of her blue blouse. It was a uniform of the German Youth organization, and he tossed it aside. Adam's tee shirt was of no use as well. Kirsten pulled her skirt down over her thighs. Her legs opened and Adam forgot everything. He was making love for the first time, drowning in a delirium of completely unknown senses. The action of their hips was synchronized as if some higher power had taught them the secret of mankind. Later, they lay and watched the stars, holding hands in silence.

They did not even look at the time when they got back. It was not even clear how they missed the evening activities without notice. But Adam could not sleep that night. He lay on the top bunk, staring at the ceiling, still feeling the swaying of Kirsten's body. That summer he discovered the symptoms of love, and together he and Kirsten excitedly planned the next possible time they could have together. It was a full year before they could see each other again.

"Comrade Hovorka wants to talk to you," the young receptionist at the Art Academy said, trying to appear as if she knew about everything that was going on.

Adam walked down the corridor, where some new student work hung. He had applied to study at the Art Academy, but the letter he had received gave no indication whether or not he had been admitted. He found a door with the Dean's name on a brass plate.

"You are Keller, Adam Keller?" asked the tall, skinny man, standing at the window.

"Yes."

"Have a seat," Hovorka prompted him. "Do you want to know why I asked you to come here?"

"Well, I'm curious," said Adam. He knew he was speaking with the unofficial god of Social Realism, and the official boss of the artists' unions. Hovorka was the Caesar of official propaganda art, holding his thumb up or down to decide on the destiny of many artists in Czechoslovakia.

"I want to have a small conversation with you, one that stays among these walls, you understand?" asked Hovorka.

Adam was silent. His throat felt dry, as if air was missing from the inventory list of the room's content.

"You are talented, very talented. We have only a few students that come close. But you have no chance of becoming a student here. Do you know that we have information about your activities?" Hovorka's words were like deadly blows to the chin.

"What activities?" tried Adam, but his voice sounded like bubbles from the small fish tank that sat on a table near the tall bookshelves.

"You will never get accepted here, because you will never be approved by the Party," Hovorka said with a pause. "So I recommend that you withdraw your application and try the Technical Institute. There is a chance that they will accept you at the School of Architecture, according to your results."

Adam did not intend to study Architecture, but he kept silent.

"Do you understand? You are wasting your time."

The message was very clear. Get out and don't bother. Adam backed out of the office, thanking Hovorka, as if for some favor he had not granted. It was an awkward situation, but soon it was over. A week later, Adam applied to the Technical Institute, requesting admission to the School of Architecture. Based on his grade point average, he was accepted.

It was July, the last summer before college. Adam wanted to enjoy freedom, even if it was just in Hungary. He was still very much in love in spite of the distance and the twelve months that had passed since he last saw Kirsten. There was good news: Kirsten and her family were on their way from East Germany. Adam was supposed to meet her in Tihanyi, a small town on Lake Balaton. He first went to visit his Uncle Gabor in Budapest, where he consumed several lunches and dinners of delicious Szegedi gulasz, stuffed peppers, and Palacsinkas, which were special crepes with jam and whipped crème. He loved his Hungarian family and their urban chutzpa that was sweet and enriching. It gave him an idea of who he could become if he would listen to their advice. But his beloved Kirsten was approaching their meeting place, so he boarded a train that would bring him to his lover. Did they still both feel the same or had she changed? He often asked himself that question, even though the letters they exchanged indicated that her feelings had not subsided.

The Hungarian countryside is flat, hot, and dusty. It is called the Puszta, a savanna-like land with wild horses, some cattle, crops, and an occasional well. Adam's head was spinning as he watched the landscape pass through the train window. He was a kid and a grownup, both categories ready for a boxing fight. Life had given him a chance to be independent more or less by default. He was not seeking it, life just threw its surprises at him and he had the choice to swim or drown.

The heat was radiating from inside the compartments and the only refuge seemed to be the open window along the long corridor. Standing in the narrow passageway Adam imagined where he would be if the Communists had not taken over the Eastern Bloc. His dreams took him to distant cities, foreign universities, and exotic islands full of romance. He shook his head and he was back on the local train to Lake Balaton. The roof of the railway car felt like an upside-down frying pan and it was just morning. The train sped through the flat lands and the air in the distance quivered, creating strange mirages. It almost looked like a lake in a distance. The coal engine hissed angrily. Adam imagined Kirsten, and the thought of his lips touching hers made his heart pound faster. Would she be there? There was no way to check.

The train made a reluctant stop in Tihanyi. Finally Adam got out, his shirt featuring maps of sweat. His backpack was quite heavy, mostly stuffed with clothes and food. His small tent was the heaviest thing he carried, and his sleeping bag was rolled up on top of the pile. A small folded easel with brushes and paint tubes also occupied half of the backpack. An old Spanish guitar with nylon strings was wrapped in a military green canvas cover and hung by his side. His guitar was Adam's closest companion. He rarely went anywhere without it, creating an appearance of a tramp. Once he was off the train he looked for shade to sit down and create a plan. Many people were passing by with evident purpose, whatever it might have been. Working on portraits of people that he knew, Adam had developed a fast eye for various types of human beings. He sat in the shade of a tree, trying to determine if most Hungarians were against the regime. They seemed content and busy, going about their business as Adam watched.

The train departed again and Adam's body cooled down enough to leave the shade. Weak Hungarian beer took away his thirst and he found a hostel for students that cost just a few Forints. It was close to the center of Tihanyi, right above a bakery. The smell of fresh bread was splendid. Adam bought half a bread loaf and ate most of it without anything else. He left his backpack in his room at the hostel and returned to the train station to check on the arrival of the international train from Germany. It had a delay.

Life is never on schedule. Or maybe we do not see it the way of the Universe. It must be proprietary information, or something of that nature. Events come unannounced. People die without notice. Children are born to the wrong parents and love fades away. Money can be found on the street. Money can be lost, the blood of civilization. Adam's grandma once said life without money is like an ape in the jungle with just a bare bosom to its name. Adam laughed, thinking of it.

The train from East Germany was painted a light mustard color and the words "Deutsche Bahn" were written in large black letters on each car. The train was full of overheated travelers, and when it stopped they spilled out onto the hot concrete. There were so many people and piles of suitcases that Adam was not sure he would find Kirsten. Then he noticed the wavy blond hair and the smile he knew so well. Kirsten was already giggling; her smile was something permanently bonded to her personality.

"You're here," she whispered and they both smiled like happy children. Kirsten's parents were happy to meet him and all the usual greetings were exchanged. Adam and Kirsten were already chatting as they carried the bags towards the center of town. They forgot about the heat, and they lost their sense of place. They continued their conversation as if the past year had only been a day. After dropping off their bags at the hotel, Kirsten asked her parents if she could go out for a walk.

It was a beautiful evening at Lake Balaton. Adam and Kirsten walked to the beach along houses facing the setting sun. The lake front was a boulevard with gigantic chestnut trees and a path of coarse sand. The villas they passed were built by Hungarian industrialists forty years before, and later seized by the Communist apparatchiks. Though they were still beautiful, many of them stood there, deteriorating in despair.

Adam put his arm around Kirsten's shoulders. "I can't believe you're here," he said. "You look older, kind of taller."

Kirsten made a sound of agreement. She always spoke less and thought more, but her smile did not leave her face. "I am going to attend the university. I will be staying in Berlin now," she said.

"I am in the Technical Institute, School of Architecture."

"Not the Art Academy?"

"No, it was naïve to think I could get in. The dean told me I had met the talent requirements, but I didn't have the right family history. You know, workers-cum-Communists and all that crap."

"It is the same in our country. I'm tired of pretending this and pretending that, saying one thing and thinking another. After a while, you become this double thinking idiot with a parallel conscience."

"It's all just propaganda," sighed Adam.

At the end of the boulevard he turned to Kirsten and hugged her closer. The sun was setting and the lake was still. Everything was so still that one could hear multiple conversations from the villas. The lovers did not hear a thing. They became one like a tangled root of a tree washed onto shore. Their kisses found new meaning. Kirsten's long hair tickled Adam's face and her breath was delightful. They sat in a boat that had washed onto shore, as if their journey was about to begin. Neither of them guessed the depth of their closeness or the separation to come. For the moment their bodies were the only reality. Kirsten sat with her back to Adam. He hugged her as if teaching her some ancient secrets. It was dark already, time for heading back.

The morning brought all the nice smells from the

bakery below. Adam was hungry and he wanted to see Kirsten again. He went downstairs and bought brioche pastries with strawberry jam and a bottle of milk to chase them down. He ate his breakfast as he walked to the hotel to meet Kirsten. They spent the day on the beach covered in suntan oil, eating salami sandwiches, and drinking cola. In the afternoon they found privacy in the small room above the bakery. Making love while people were buying fresh bread turned out to be a romantic idea. Kneading fresh dough and caressing breasts. Kirsten tried to be silent, with mixed success. The baking women smiled as they heard the familiar sounds.

Adam had never before felt so free and happy. This kind of freedom, however temporary, was feeding his hungry soul. It was freedom of the moment, fleeting and ephemeral. Yet love builds foundations of something stronger. A rudimentary kinship. Adam and Kirsten's conversations slowly turned more and more political, analytical, and critical of the regimes they were suffering under. They found many similarities between the two Communist countries. Neither of them could travel to the western countries because the capitalist world was deemed a threat. Most people did not have much money since their governments purposely kept everyone close to poverty level so that no luxuries could be enjoyed. It kept people working, not thinking.

Both governments also controlled who was able to study, and what school was decided appropriate for each individual. The biggest concern was that all the rules applied to the common man, not to the privileged Communists. The apparatchiks had things like yogurt from Switzerland, fish from Sweden, and other exceptions, like travel privileges. Almost everyone else lived in communal apartments made of concrete and shaped into uniform boxes promoting mediocrity. Even the ceiling height was regulated at a low height to keep people depressed at all times. While most people endured these conditions, the privileged few were living in villas like the one seized from Adam's family, traveling to the West, and eating exotic food. "All men are born equal, except some are more equal than others," Adam joked to Kirsten with Orwellian humor.

Their conversations cut short by time, two weeks of love and sunshine flew away fast. Adam and Kirsten came up with a plan to meet in Berlin over winter break. The last kiss before Adam's train left was the hottest, leaving them branded for the long winter to come.

Part Two

Berlin
1979

After Adam passed all his tests and exams he boarded a train with a destination written on a metal plate that hung on the side of each car: Berlin. Again, he felt that magnetic attraction and the thrill of the unknown. It was asking Adam to be curious, impatient, explorative, and impulsive. He was in the vortex again, wondering if he was the cause of events, or if he was only acting them out as they were scripted.

The train was dirty and noisy. Adam had to cope with the black railroad dust and the smoke from the engines. The green, patent leather compartments were all empty. It was wintertime and travelers to Berlin did not find a sunny Riviera there. Adam counted thirty-five people in the entire train, each one taking over three seats in order to sleep during their eleven hour trip. Sleeper cars were available but they weren't affordable for a student who had to support himself. He found an empty compartment and threw his backpack on one seat and his coat on another. It was wise to wait for the train conductor to stop and punch his ticket before pulling the curtains together to sleep until they reached Prague. The ride turned out to be cozy and no one bothered him, but to be safe Adam put his valuable passport and money under his body so that it would be impossible to rob him in his sleep.

Border crossing was intimidating and stressful. Even though this was only an East Bloc border between the two Communist countries, the guards deemed travelers guilty until proven otherwise. At least it felt like that. Arguably, border crossings were the best places for the Communist power to manifest itself, baring its teeth as if the enemy was at the gates. The enemy *was* at the gates, only it was the border guards who were the enemy as they intimidated travelers with their machine guns.

The truth was that even perfectly innocent people felt guilty and frightened when they crossed the borders, especially those who had never smuggled anything nor lied about the content of their baggage. The prevalent paranoia made the days of the Communist rule gloomy. Adam wondered how entire countries had become big jails. How did one's freedom to move from place to place become illegal?

The Communist mob that took over Czechoslovakia in 1949 in a so called political victory, started out by nationalizing wealth. Nationalizing meant that what was yours became someone else's. Not very many seized properties ever saw the light as a National property, which would at least have been within the utopian party lines. Instead it was the apparatchiks who suddenly lived like kings. They put the former land owners, industrial-ists, barons, and countesses out on the street. For a short period of time some were allowed to leave, and the smart ones did just that. They chose Switzerland, Germany, Austria, or even the United States.

After a while, the borders were shut tight with barbed wire. Guards were trained to shoot anyone that came within the vicinity of the border. Jails were filled with political inmates who disagreed with Stalin's ideology. The Communist disciples became holier than the pope and local leaders implemented strict laws to protect the regime. It was a proven method: first you take away civil rights. Then you start punishing even the smallest resistance. Intimidate every person that speaks up against the regime. Make sure the population is kept in poverty, then declare a common enemy. It is a recipe for a totalitarian government.

Adam definitely felt anxious as he was scrutinized by the border guards. He saw grim faces, sharp orders, and the uncertainty of not knowing if his passport would be returned. All of this happened in the middle of the night, with a few German Shepherds for intimidation. The dark sky outside was illuminated by yellow security lights that shone down on the lifeless environment around the crossing. Nothing but dirty train tracks with black oil stains between the rails.

After all the suitcases were turned upside-down and inside-out, Adam felt the train rolling again. They continued their journey to Berlin, the city with one name but two countries. Divided by a wall of concrete, epitomizing the status quo of the times, like a cold war in a can. The Third Reich had burned down only to give birth to a bizarre chapter of modern civilization. One nation speaking a common language, yet divided so that brother could not visit sister, families split in half. That was the status of the East and West Berlin. And somewhere in there, a young German girl was waiting for her best friend.

⤳

The train came to a screeching stop. Adam was tired after the long night, but his excitement had taken over as soon as dawn arrived. As they got closer he watched the countryside change from snowy fields into a more urban setting, until finally tall buildings surrounded the tracks. Someone yelled, "Caffe, Fruhstuck," but Adam didn't think he would be able to swallow anything. His mind raced with memories mixed with expectations. It was certainly natural to imagine the meeting with Kirsten, but his brain was still in a haze. It was foggy outside too. Adam opened the window, but quickly shut it when the cold air rushed in. Shivers made him pull a sweater over his head and indulge in the thick wool his grandma had knitted for him.

There was a small crowd in the train. German citizens must have embarked after the border Adam thought. Many of them were working in Berlin and they used the train to commute to work. Adam made sure he did not leave anything in his compartment and moved towards the exit. The Bahnhof was crowded as he started to look for Kirsten. Bumping into people, he made his way to the center of the large train station.

Sounds are truly unique to the railway stations. A cacophony of mechanical noises mixed with human voices and amplified announcements. A couple of minutes felt like an hour as Adam looked at every face he passed in order to find the familiar one. When people do not see each other for a long period of time they start imagining how the other might look different. It is hard

54

to be sure. The clothes made it even harder, and fashion changed overnight.

Finally his eyes recognized Kirsten. She did not see him until he almost stood beside her. "Ah, Mein Gott, Adam, hier bist Du!"

"You're here," Adam said. Then they stood silent, just smiling. For a whole minute they just stared at each other, with soft smiles stamped on their radiant faces. They realized that they were almost alone. All the people had cleared the platform and only a grumpy train station employee was coughing nervously to get them moving and clear his assigned area. The comrade was probably waiting for the end of his shift.

"Shall we go?" Adam asked as he picked up his backpack.

"I have so many plans for us," Kirsten said excitedly.

"Great, I promise to stay however long you want," Adam said. Then he thought that this promise was silly. He had a maximum of two weeks of break.

The young couple didn't think about that anymore as they exited the train station and headed out to find a street car. Adam was not paying attention to the world around him. He was enjoying his guide and hung on every one of her words. Observant as he was, he noticed that Kirsten had become a city girl with a metropolitan flair. He wasn't sure quite what it was. It could have been her long wool winter coat, or the white shawl she wore over it. Or the nonchalance in all her moves. Adam's thoughts were soon replaced with a single thought: it was becoming bitterly cold. Berlin was all white with fresh snow. It was still early in the morning, but the city was already bustling with samples of society. The thing that united them was the visible breath condensing in front of everyone's mouths. Glancing at the gloomy buildings around them, Adam saw a slogan covering half a building façade: *Proletariats from around the world, unite.* It was clear that no one took care to maintain the dilapidating real estate. It was as if the black and white images from the end of the war had come to life. People amidst crumbling buildings, clinging to their few possessions wrapped in jute bags. Except now, the jute bags were replaced by plastic bags with advertising logos from various retailers. Plastic bags were the prized possessions of the Communist world, and the cheap bags the Western department stores liked to give away with purchases were now used as high fashion. People collected those modern icons and kept them in good condition, carrying them around like purses.

Ownership, ownership, and again, ownership, flashed through Adam's mind. The street car finally materialized from around the corner with a screeching sound that was typical in European cities and they piled in with the frozen crowd. The street car found its way through wide boulevards designed by the noted architect Schinkel. The street car made a stop at the Schauspiel-haus Theatre, but the young lovers were still cozy sitting in public transportation with free heat. Slowly, the crowd receded and the streets became different. More and more buildings were damaged as if World War II had just ended a few months ago. Windows with broken glass, paint peeling from the buildings, and remnants of poster scraps hung from concrete walls. They passed occasional corner stores with customers that could remember Adolf Hitler. Kirsten pointed them out to

Adam on several snowy streets. As they approached their destination, the buildings looked like a scene from an old movie. They exited the streetcar and their boots touched down on the sidewalk, leaving footprints in the fresh snow like the first moon landing. Soon, the tram turned the corner and there was silence.

"It's not far from here," Kirsten said, seeing Adam's inquisitive look. "I live in an abandoned apartment. No one wanted it, so I fixed it, and it's fine now. I live there kind of free. It's not official, but nobody seems to mind."

They approached a strange building. The front façade was dark grey, almost black. The huge portal took a good part of the frontage. The wood gate was at least fourteen feet tall and it had seen better days. A small door was a part of the bigger door but on separate hinges, and it was locked. It was obvious that the large gate had not been used for at least thirty years.

Kirsten opened the door after checking around for onlookers. There was no one around, but it was habitual. Since the Stasi secret police ran the country trust was not in most people's vocabularies.

The building had a large inner courtyard. This was typical for pre-war apartment buildings, and the courtyards added ventilation and light to some rooms at the core. Part of the building looked normal, but the rear side was for all intents and purposes a legal ruin. Bricks were scattered around and only two stories remained standing. The rest was just a memory after a bomb hit it sometime in the spring of 1945. Kirsten led them through a long hallway, turned left, and opened a door. It was the space directly under the ruin.

Kirsten's apartment legally did not exist. After the

British bomb hit the roof, it did not make it into the register of apartments because it was sitting under a pile of rubble. But as Berlin was becoming more and more populated, some entrepreneurial student cleared just enough rubble to expose the windows to the fresh air and placed old roof tiles over the apartment above to protect the broken building from rain. That was the rebirth of a studio used by friends of friends, mostly students of Humboldt University. No one had to pay rent and electric power was rigged to common maintenance areas like the hallways and the now useless elevator. This situation, somewhat unimaginable for the rest of the world, was normal under the conditions of Communist Berlin, where most lived in fear and common people minded their own business.

Kirsten turned on the light, and a magical world appeared in front of Adam's eyes. One large room with a kitchenette near the window, tall ceilings, and a tiled stove that was radiating heat. The room was warm and inviting, bathed in the soft light from a ceiling chandelier. This unbelievable secret world was furnished partly with someone's original furniture, completed with found and recycled pieces of various origins. The wood floor was painted burgundy red, the wide planks happy to be providing comfort after so many years of disrepair.

"What do you think?" Kirsten asked, interrupting the silence.

"Is this where you live? I did not imagine it would be this...special." Adam revealed his surprise. Kirsten was already stoking the stove with bricks of coal. Adam thought her practicality was undoubtedly linked to her intelligence.

"This is the only heat we have," she said. "The chimney was left standing without any damage."

Adam helped close the cast iron doors of the stove, examining the remarkable tile that covered its entire height. The corners were done with an ornamental panache, and every piece was handmade, with relief ornaments creating the faint image of a room with beams. Kirsten turned around and they locked in embrace, staring into each others' eyes for a moment before they kissed. Her perfume was as mysterious as her entire presence in this surreal setting. They tumbled into the bathroom, taking off clothes piece by piece. Adam did not remember how they turned on the shower, but he realized he was standing in a claw footed tub under an antique shower head, surrounded by a linen curtain. The couple was covered in soap bubbles from head to toes. They did not stop kissing, making the bath foreplay of sorts, even though Adam needed a good shower after his hours of travel.

The water was hot from another stove, a very small coal-burning water heater, and the temperature started to decline before too long, reminding them to wash off quickly. By the time they were done with the shower, the water was ice cold. They dried their bodies with a towel, and shivering, found their place under the big down comforter. Kirsten's nipples were hard from the cold water, but her kisses were hot. Adam was still shivering with passion and excitement. He naturally found his position between her legs and she navigated him inside her wet paradise. They made love for hours and Kirsten's face burned like the coal inside the stove. "Mein Schatz," she whispered.

Later, they lay on their backs, hands intertwined in some cubistic art form, as they daydreamed about freedom. As they had a thousand times before, they verbalized a utopia where everyone had a right to decide things for themselves, where no one was watched, and no one was imprisoned for having different ideas. All this dreaming could have possibly been unrealistic or illusionary. But they did not know that; how could they? They did not know that happiness was right next to them, with them all along, that they were touching it with a sensuality only known to lovers.

All of a sudden, they found hunger, or hunger found them. Kirsten had a German breakfast in mind, so she whipped out scrambled eggs, warmed buns, and served butter, ham, and eggs. Beside the plates she set jam, honey, and tea, all with a smile. It was a very late lunch, after which they took off into the streets. Kirsten had a whole plan prepared for Adam's visit. First they wanted to see all the museums. Some of the greatest museums found themselves in the East Berlin, even as the Wall slowly grew around them. Adam and Kirsten hurried off together, content to talk for hours.

The following days were filled with cultural explorations. They made love all evening and most mornings, then surfaced only briefly for food and air like whales. Kirsten's wild, naturally blond hair was one of the things that imprints into a man's memory forever. Adam already knew he could never forget her.

A week passed and the thrill of being together did not subside. By the second week into Adam's visit however, Kirsten had revealed much of her disgruntlement with the things and events around her. She was clearly over the edge of being just marginally unhappy with the regime, and she was no longer pleased about being a part of the puppetry. At times she boiled over with her regime-bashing speeches, taking no prisoners in her argument. With Adam though she was only preaching to the choir. Yet he was still caught by surprise when she revealed a plan to escape. It was even more unexpected news when she told him she was ready to leave now.

Kirsten whispered words of conspiracy while they pretended to look at timeless pieces of ancient art from the Greek temples that had been hoarded by Schliemann and other German explorers. The bodies of warriors, frozen in painful poses, waiting to slay the enemy or be slaughtered themselves, witnessed the plans Kirsten had already made as she gave the details to Adam. Chariots and horses stopped in full gallop and looked at them, trying to lip read the secrets of her plan to leave everything behind. It became clearer with every word that she was serious. Kirsten was connected to an underground group that was arranging illegal crossings into West Berlin. It was basically a business that arranged the covert smuggling of people over the Wall for profit. A dangerous proposition, at the very least. Adam's head was spinning, and he got almost dizzy thinking about his family back in Bratislava. How could he possibly leave them without saying good byes? Or the alternative—saying good bye to his love?

Adam's mind was racing to make sense of the situation, however unprepared he was. He was in love with this beautiful and strong woman beyond any doubt. But was he prepared to cut all ties to the world he was a part of? Was he ready to take that ultimate step? However familiar he was with the world in exile, it was all indirect, like Milan Kundera's novels or the Velvet Underground and Karel Kryl's songs. He imagined the world on the other side of the fences, but he was hardly ready. On the other hand, there is no soft way to do this kind of thing. It was death if they caught you.

After two days and a sleepless night, tense with discussions about the pros and cons, Adam decided to go. He agreed to join the group of eight young people determined to make the crossing even though he had no idea how the plan worked, nor did Kirsten. The technical part of it was a secret only the group's guide knew. The blueprints for escapes were different with each case. People attempted to walk through forests, flew homemade balloons or crop dusting planes, swam across rivers, dug tunnels, sailed through the rough waters of the Baltic Sea, or simply climbed over the

Wall. Many died. Many were caught and imprisoned in-definitely. If they made it, their families were persecuted and lost any place in the society they once had. The secret police seized all the possessions of any defectors, routinely followed by interrogations of their family members, making it harder for anyone else to commit such a crime. Guilt and imposed responsibility was too hard to take.

Adam struggled with all of this, and yet he was not afraid for his life. Most of the time he still felt invincible, and beyond that there was not much he would lose in the way of earthly treasures. His family was dear to him, but he felt certain he could help them from a distance. He and Kirsten packed the essential documents they needed along with a few clothes, and locked the apartment. They left the key under a loose brick as an invitation for others to take over their secret world.

They caught a tram to get to the covert meeting place. They knew only two other people and the guy that was the connection to the main guide. Kirsten knew half a dozen people that had successfully made it to the other side by following the same guide. She even talked to them from a phone booth, avoiding any names. Details or facts spoken aloud could be incriminating. They were all safe in West Berlin, that was all the proof she needed. Adam felt a strange current that carried them in a direction they no longer controlled. He felt that once he jumped in, he had to hold on strong to resurface somewhere alive. Things were again moving in a vortex.

They got off the tram somewhere in Pankow. It was past midnight, and they tried to look like late night party goers, lost in a district Adam was truly unfamiliar with. The night was bitterly cold, but neither of them felt the temperature because their adrenaline was pumping overtime. Kirsten found the address where they were supposed to meet the guide. The six others were already on the spot. Adam vaguely knew two of them and he mumbled hello. No one was in the mood for chatting. Silence lasted for what seemed an eternity. Then a man in his thirties arrived and it was clear he was the guide. Adam examined him for a few seconds. He was a short, muscular guy with curly dark hair, not typical for a German. He had a small backpack, and by his movements Adam could feel his energy. His instructions were simple, he was in charge. "Synchronize your watches. Tighten the straps on your backpacks. Tie your shoe laces and follow me," he said.

They walked behind him, then almost ran through a few inner courtyards and arcades. Before crossing an empty street, the guide examined the surrounding area and motioned for the group to follow. Finally, after a maze of hallways and arcades, they climbed two flights of stairs and entered an unheated apartment. All this happened in darkness, illuminated only by a full moon that peeked from behind the clouds over the dark buildings.

"Take this in both hands and do not let go," the guide whispered. Each person was handed a tool that looked like a hollow metal circle with a triangular handle attached. The handle was a bent pipe that had a duct tape for its grip. A belt with a buckle hung off the metal contraption. Adam did not comprehend all of it, but he observed others and watched the guide closely.

The guide motioned them to an opened window. He gestured toward a cable that was anchored on the windowsill and stretched out into the dark space outside. Adam caught a glimpse of the Wall. They were quite close to it.

Before Adam could say anything to Kirsten, the first person had already attached his wheel to the cable. The guide tightened the belt around the person's waist and helped him step out of the window. They lost the sight of him in an instant. Next was another girl, then Kirsten. The guide began to show signs of anxiety; something was not right. The moon peeked from behind the clouds, illuminating the scene. But what was clearly disturbing the guide was the sound of the rolling wheel on the cable. It was a screeching sound, cutting the silence of the night like a razor as Adam watched Kirsten slide out the window into the darkness.

There was a sudden and silent explosion of search lights, piercing the darkness with might of a samurai sword. They heard voices shouting orders and dogs barking. Before Adam could attach his reel, the guide suddenly released the cable from its anchor. It disappeared into the night, like a hissing snake. The others were already running down the stairs, leaving Adam no choice but to follow as fast as he could. The group surged through the back door to the alley, then someone turned left and the rest followed. The empty street was covered with ice and patches of ashes. At the end of the street behind them, vehicle headlights appeared. Adam heard the sounds of dogs being released as he followed the guys in front of him. A couple of blocks down the alley someone opened a window on the ground floor. They jumped in. It was not high above the ground, yet it was difficult to see, and Adam landed hard on his wrist. The window was shut behind them and the group ran through another courtyard onto another street. This time they ran towards a park fence. They climbed over, just in time to escape the headlights of a turning vehicle. It was a GAZ, a type of Soviet military jeep that was used by the armed forces all around the Eastern Bloc.

Behind them the dogs jumped against the fence that was too high for them. The vehicle was also at a standstill, and obviously the soldiers were not in the mood to jump fences. Adam could hear his heart pounding like a drum. He was in good shape, yet he was gasping for air. The park provided enough cover and soon they emerged on the other side where there was another group of people waiting for a late night tram. Adam realized that the group had been split up as he saw the last person walk off towards the entrance to a bar. He saw a tram turn a corner and he jumped on as it came to a stop. The sweat was streaming down his cheeks, dripping off his chin, but there were only a few drunks inside the tram, and the driver did not seem to care.

Ten minutes later, Adam started to recognize the buildings and he could make out the district. It was relatively close to Kirsten's apartment. Where was Kirsten? She had been the last one out. Had she made it?

Adam was in a state of shock, but his life saving skills kicked in. He found the loose brick where Kirsten had left the key, got inside the apartment, and locked the door behind him. He slid down to the cold floor in silence. The only thing he kept hearing was his own heartbeat. There was no way to count the minutes Adam sat on the floor behind the door. The uninterrupted silence suggested that he was safe from harm. For the moment at least. He felt unable to move. He sat there, paralyzed, until he felt the cold floor. The stove was also cold, and Adam gathered old newspapers to start a fire. There were only a few bricks of coal left, but it was more than enough for the few hours he might stay. When he finally got the fire going, he tried to sort out the situation in his mind. Kirsten was gone. He started to cry, and he couldn't stop shaking. He was devastated and afraid.

After a while, Adam gathered all his belongings and packed his large backpack. He had no money left because he had given all of it to Kirsten to pay for the guide. He had a valid, round-trip ticket to Bratislava and there was nothing holding him back. As soon as the dawn came, he locked the apartment and placed the key under the brick again. Sooner or later, someone would replace them.

Adam arrived to the train station early and joined a crowd of people waiting for the train to arrive. Soon the train pulled into the station for early boarding. No one seemed to be interfering, so Adam took his place in a compartment with other travelers. He pretended to read some newspaper he found on a bench. He kept reassuring himself that no one could possibly know about their attempt to escape. The crowd provided a good cover. He looked just like hundreds of other students traveling for school break. Even if the Stasi had followed him and Kirsten at times, the events of the night before evaporated with the daylight, like the steam from the hot dogs at the railway station.

Adam still felt tense all the way to the border. His heart pounded again as the border guards checked his belongings, even though he didn't have anything incriminating. Already Kirsten was only a memory. The train station in Prague was extremely crowded. Adam felt numb to the outside world.

Kirsten felt the cold air on her face. She grabbed the handle on the contraption while the guide attached the safety belt around her waist. She stepped into the darkness. The ride on a makeshift zip line was short, yet it felt like an eternity. Half way down, the watch tower lights came on. The search lights did not find her, but they were frantically looking. As she approached the other side someone grabbed her to bring her to a stop. The two other people that had jumped before her were there. She noticed a few other figures as the lights illuminated the grounds. All of a sudden the cable came loose and fell on the ground. She tried to look for Adam, but the small group was ready to leave. Kirsten wanted them to stop but they needed to get away from the vicinity of the Wall. There was a commotion on the other side. The watch towers were lit up with search lights in action. Dogs barked into the night.

The group walked to a van parked on a street around the corner. Kirsten did not want to leave without Adam, but it became clear that he had not made it. She got in the van with several rows of seats, most of them empty. It had obviously been organized for more people. The van turned the corner and a few minutes later it took them through sparkling streets with storefront windows lit up as if they were in a dream from a Western movie. It was hard to believe they were still in Berlin. The colors were the first and obvious sign of her new freedom. Everything was so much more colorful, bright, and clean. When she finally got her voice back she asked the strangers what had just happened.

"They had to cut the line. The pigs heard us. They had to run," one of the guys informed her.

"Scheisse," she replied. What else was there to say?

"You three will all be staying together for the night," said a blond man in a leather jacket. "Tomorrow we will go to the police. It is standard procedure."

The van pulled into an alley, then into a subterranean garage. They walked up to an apartment that was furnished sparely, yet functionally. In the warmth of the central heating, Kirsten's mind melted like the clocks in Salvador Dali's painting. Going back to East Berlin was just as good as suicide, and yet losing Adam felt unbearable. She could hardly sleep and the morning came very fast. Two guys came back to the apartment with some food from a bakery, and made coffee. Better than the muddy excuse for coffee in East Berlin, she thought. The three escapees had already showered and the breakfast was well appreciated. They got ready to leave and report their arrival to the local police. All of this was hard to distinguish from a wild dream. Kirsten's sense of reality had drowned in the darkness from the night before. The morning just prolonged this strange experience. She followed instructions and went through the motions. It was the only thing she could do.

Part Three
Slovakia-Czech Republic
1979-1987

7

*B*ack in Bratislava, things were not much different from when Adam had left. He realized that no one had any idea about his failed attempt to escape. He had come close to getting caught, but the fact remained that he hadn't been and there was no incriminating evidence about his experience in Berlin. At least it appeared that way. If he kept his mouth shut he was safe, he reasoned. He picked up the pieces of his life and put it together fast. Everyone was very happy to see him and no one seemed to notice anything different in his mood or in his demeanor.

His friend and mentor Stevo was the only one Adam confided in. They discussed the consequences of Kirsten's escape and for Adam the dust finally settled. At least on the surface. Deep in his mind, the memories lingered and images popped up at night, robbing him of his sleep. Like a tape playing over and over in a loop, he saw images of the streets of Berlin, frozen in some artistic stills, refusing to vacate the hallways of his mind. Deep inside there was an aftermath, a new day after conflict, the battlefield covered with bodies. But on the surface, things resumed.

School started and life got back on track. The school of architecture proved to be more and more interesting, with each semester revealing new knowledge to the young minds. Adam learned to like it; with every new assignment a fresh sheet of paper provoked his creative mind and he attacked the challenges with growing confidence. After school friends met to discuss well worn topics and new political gossip kept them busy. Adam still hoped to hear something from Kirsten and he checked the mailbox every day for a postcard or a letter. After a while he finally stopped looking.

<hr />

Nothing feels more real than something that hurts. In the early eighties, when the dust from the Russian tanks finally settled, Czechoslovakia had become a very organized prison. Its walls were barbed wire fences at every border and the secret police played the guards. It was a tragic comedy with an edge of Dostoevsky.

In the spring of 1983, communism was still hanging tough like a broken zipper. Food was sparse, yet the supply was better than in Romania or Russia. Although somewhat monochromatic, life was essentially livable as long as you did not poke your nose into politics, strive for some form of higher consciousness, or desire the luxury of open philosophical conversations. You could even eat meat if you were willing to stand in endless lines for the limited supply, and people had small gardens to grow every possible vegetable in their own yards. Yet corruption flourished. Everyone needed to know some genie in a position to grant them access to more—because there was always something better or sweeter, as long as the price was paid.

There was an unwritten schedule of bribes and barters available to navigate one's way through the valleys of communism in Czechoslovakia. Access to Western movies was one of the privileges many kept quiet for. Access to books was an advantage of another small group. Being more privileged was a goal, and a rather ironic game in the supposedly equal society.

Adam hated the corruption. It reminded him of something Orwellian and it never felt good to him to play that game. Many people believed that when in Rome they needed to play as the Romans did. The need for essential supplies and services created an unprecedented market for knowing the right people, never mind the dangers of getting caught trading korunas for Western dollars or German Marks—what many knew as the "real" currencies. Sink or swim, everyone had to find their groove. Adam was happy to know some people that were giving away treasures in troves. Not in diamonds and gold, but rather something better than that. For Adam, forbidden literature created a world of multidimensional qualities. A "tour d' intellect" without a passport.

Again and again, writers like Solzeniczin targeted the perpetual lies of the Communist regime and gave Adam the badly needed confirmation of what he held as truth. Even if he wasn't physically, his mind felt very free. He thought of how the infamous Vladimir Ilyich Lenin paraphrased Confucius with a statement that freedom is just in the mind. A free mind delivers a free body. For Adam, freedom was all kind of things, such as staring at the Communist slogans on cheap billboards while laughing inside. Freedom was the ability to listen to Communist lectures at school and read George Orwell under the desk. Freedom was knowing about other viewpoints and sharing them with friends. But the ideologues were always watching. Everywhere. Once you began to think differently, you were different, and Big Brother watches those that are different. He is watching you right now.

Adam was definitely different. He had established a wonderful world of friends and dissidents that could laugh as a group in the face of official propaganda and be free together. With them it felt natural to be able to talk from one's heart, easy talk that felt like uncovering the truth. Long evenings of conversations were healing. It wasn't long before the entire group around Adam had developed a dangerous habit of expressing open, uncensored ideas. There was a present and looming danger of getting comfortable and casual about their double-thought process. Adam was becoming increasingly bold about his views and his pro-Western attitudes. Especially after his experience at the Berlin Wall, he was much less careful in concealing his thoughts. He made signs to the Universe that could be described as a middle finger pointed towards the sky. It came as no surprise that his personal files at the secret police archives were growing thicker.

Free education was one of the rare gifts that the Communist regime had left in place for its people. Of course, nothing is free and people paid a big price for the opportunity to have access to higher education without paying tuition. The government took advantage of the cheap labor, paying people a pittance for their work. But in spite of a propaganda-loaded curriculum, there was vast knowledge to feed on. Adam had learned a great deal about architecture, structures, design, and history. At the same time, the theoretical knowledge did not make one an architect, ready for the real world's fights over projects, fees, and clients. It barely made him aware of what was to come. And in the background there was always his ultimate passion for all things artistic, for painting and sculpture, and for the mystery of creating magic.

The concept of luck versus diligence is as old as mankind itself. Yet it can be puzzling to watch the masters deliver the real deal. Adam wondered how they developed the skills, knowledge, and talent. Were the best of the best born with their talent? Was it destiny? Was talent a fully developed advantage inherited from the gods? Adam felt it was clear that his biggest talent was forcing him to be an artist. This force, irresistible like a woman's charm, was as unavoidable as a seductive lover. Architecture did not speak to him with the same power, even though it was a pleasant diversion. Yet the question of destiny can not be answered easily. Adam thought of the case of Sallicri and Mozart. One was destined to be the love child of the gods. The other was fated to become a jealous follower, very talented, but not the chosen one. Who writes the script for those roles, Adam wondered. He wanted to see the backstage.

During the last couple of years in graduate school, the professors called the students their colleagues. At first it sounded mocking, as if the professors were teasing them. But slowly, everyone got used to it. By the final year many students became friends with their teachers, spending more time with them in pubs and clubs, drinking and talking. They were lovers of words, philosophers, and truth seekers. Endless story tellers, gypsies, and nomads. Adam spent many hours arguing various points of life with his professors, earning recognition for his sense of humor and fearless commentaries. Evenings brought new friends while the narrow alleys echoed with drunken monologues presented by all those anonymous philosophers. The walls of the old city heard it all.

Adam opened up to life again, breathing air and creating new art. In fact, some of the trauma from Berlin showed up in his new paintings, which friends said were as strong and expressionistic as Edward Munch's. He worked on several canvases at the same time, radically capturing political ideas. He felt uneasy about self censorship, yet there was something holding him back from unleashing his anger and spitting it all out. It was through his best friend Stevo, that Adam met another student named Zuzana and her father, a man who had dedicated his life to opposition. In Zuzana's father Adam found a source of knowledge and information about the outside world, and he and Adam spent hours analyzing developments in politics and economy.

Adam valued this knowledge of all things prohibited, countercultural, and underground. The dissident group around Zuzana's father was enticing to the young minds, particularly because of the flow of uncensored information that unveiled the dirt and the corruption of the late Communist politicians. Those were the times of KGB surveillance, and the times of the cultural underground. Adam felt himself exploding with ideas, poems, and songs that he shared with his buddies who were equally creative in similar areas.

Zuzana also became an increasing part of Stevo's life, like an anchor in the stormy seas. She was a realist, almost to the point of cynicism, and she had a very technical thinking mind. Probably influenced by her father, she saw the world in black and white colors, and most clearly for what it was not, rather than seeing the world as full of possibility. But that was the calming substance Stevo needed most. He admired what he was lacking. They often laughed at the sarcastic jokes, so common in Zuzana's family. The proclamations were stated with a smile, making the negatives strangely endearing. If Stevo was a helium balloon, she was the string tied to the stake in the ground. If he was a cloud, then she was the wind that moved him closer to the earth. The relationship changed Stevo, and Adam felt that it was the end of freedom for his mentor, but he didn't let Stevo know. It was the end of something however, and certainly the final role Stevo played in Adam's life.

And with a fresh diploma in hand, the young architects from Adam's class found themselves looking for jobs in the land of equal opportunities. Again, some were more equal than others, and Adam was among the last ones to find a firm that offered him a chair. Like everything else, the process was a theatre of the absurd. The Communist system did not promote individual qualities of the elite designers, but rather it stood for mediocrity and the suppression of ambitions. In theory, employment was a right and an obligation at the same time. Therefore thousands were formally employed in useless and ineffective companies with no projects to work on.

Adam found himself stuck with such a phony job, where work was being invented to kill time. There was nothing to design and nothing to build, but it was okay to read Pravda newspapers all morning with coffee and buns at hand. Like everything else, nothing existed unless one could invent it for himself. Adam and his friends desperately searched for possibilities. He who seeks, finds, and so the young and restless architects found a source for international design competitions in architecture. Finally, there was something to strive for in their profession. Young architects selected partners and created teams, pitched in money and purchased the competition rules. Weeks of hard work followed as they tried to make the deadline and ship their design entries. Adam scored several times in these competitions along with his other team members.

Money in foreign currency was flowing in, and Adam soon gained a reputation for good design. Still, all this was a playground where "good kids" were allowed to play. The government was watching all the players, making sure no one left the building too soon. Emigration was considered one of the biggest crimes, akin to treason. In spite of that, many people were still finding ways to escape. Yugoslavia was one of the grey area vacation spots where busses returned half empty. People literally walked to Austria through the forest, or took a boat to Italy. Adam would have done that in a flash, had it not been for an incident with the secret police.

Adam had just won a significant award for creating one of the ten best projects in a roster of two thousand world architects. He won an invitation from Japan that came with airline ticket, and pocket change of three thousand US dollars. He got so excited that he went to Prague and filed for the Japanese visa.

In a month, he was called to get his passport stamped by the Japanese Embassy. Another trip to Prague resulted in a beautiful stamp with Kanji writing in his passport. Adam then applied for the infamous Communist passport authority permit to travel. They told him to wait several weeks. Two days later there was a knock at the door of his grandmother's apartment. Men in black entered and demanded his passport. There was no way to fight and Adam had to give up his documents and his dream of seeing the world on the other side of the iron curtain. This was the ultimate disappointment, as it was the end to any kind of travel, even within the Eastern Bloc. Perhaps the East German secret police supplied materials and information to their Communist brothers in Czechoslovakia. Or someone close to Adam had written a letter to inform the secret police about a possibility of emigration. No one ever knew.

In an ironic turn of events, Adam actually did get a document forcing him to travel, only the destination was not his chosen one. He was drafted into the Czechoslovakian Army, a one year obligatory service common for young graduates. Traditionally, college graduates served in the armed forces for twelve months, learning to fire weapons and stand sentry. A few people who were on the government watch list had a different assignment. Adam had to report at a remote place in Southern Moravia, little known for anything but being just a dot in the middle of Mohelno Desert.

Within a month the boys would become soldiers.

*I*n the wee hours of the morning the train station resembled a grungy movie. The pale faces of future soldiers, barely awakened, were slumped on the benches. They were surfacing from long nights of parties and good-byes with their lovers. The government served draft papers to young men between the ages of eighteen and twenty-four unless they were deemed disabled or mentally unfit for service. In the harsh, cold light of the train station a few of these young men were talking to each other, some were sleeping on the cold floor, and many were accompanied by their mothers or girlfriends. Various trains had been announced throughout the night, their arrivals mumbled through loudspeakers in a typically incomprehensible way. The train number and the name of the destination were usually emphasized, followed by the panicky actions of men grabbing bags and suitcases and dashing towards their destiny.

Adam didn't meet anyone with the same destination that he had found typed in his letter, although some were traveling to Brno, the closest large city in the same direction. Adam finally boarded his train where he spotted another architect he knew.

"Where did they send you?" Adam asked.

"Prague," responded the architect.

"Lucky you," gasped Adam, "I am going to some god forsaken village in southern Moravia."

"Where?"

"Kramolin," Adam said, revealing an official military secret.

"Never heard of it. Hope it's not on the border. The border guards stand sentry all night long, rain or shine."

They discussed their last days of school, people they knew, and jobs they had found. They didn't talk about it, but the underlying feeling was that life was going to change and this interlude in their lives would be substantial. The trains carried more bottles of wine and Slivovica than a liquor store. Perhaps they felt it was their last chance to celebrate the scattered fractions of freedom, or perhaps the men were looking for escape. Maybe it was just the manly thing to do.

Most of the young men were traveling to a military training camp or a base with an official address for one or two years of obligatory army training. By government regulation the young men found themselves dressed in green garb, with their wings clipped short to tame their spirits and prevent their young urges to fly. At the camp they went through standard training with weapons, marching to music, and living a day at a time. However brainless, dull, and unintelligent the training seemed to be, the law provided for this theater.

Adam stepped out of his train onto the dirty tiled

surface of the Brno train station and walked towards the information booth.

"How do I get to Kramolin?" he inquired at the window.

"Are you reporting there as a new recruit?" the man at the counter asked.

"Yes, that's what my papers say."

"Well, if that's your orders, then go to the right side of the building where you'll see military vehicles. They'll take you there."

Walking and following instructions would become Adam's new life for a while. He turned left and saw the trucks with green canvas covers, with a few young men sitting high on the bench and some others smoking nearby.

Two men in uniforms stood at the wall with a smirk on their faces, looking partly bored and amused by the new recruits. Adam didn't recognize anyone so he joined an isolated guy that seemed similarly lost in the spectacle around them.

"Are we going to Kramolin?" Adam asked the man.

The guy studied Adam's face for few seconds before he replied.

"We'll end up somewhere," he said. The man's face was pale and he had dirty blond hair that fell over thin wire glasses to emphasize his intellectual appearance. He spoke Czech, and there was a slight stutter in his voice.

"I'm Marek." His hand extended forward in an official introduction.

"I'm Adam. So are we going to Kramolin?" As he spoke a voice shouted into the crowd of two dozen young men.

"This is the transport to Kramolin," the voice barked. "Everyone going to Kramolin, finish smoking and get up on the truck."

Covered with a dirty canvas, two long benches were lined up along the sides of the vehicle to seat a dozen guys on the right, and a dozen on the left. Their duffle bags landed in the middle and the truck started with a loud noise. Noise would become the norm in the times to come. There was nothing quiet in the military. The truck was no exception, and the conversations between the men stopped altogether.

The city of Brno soon disappeared, replaced by scenes of villages. Later the truck wound its way through a vast land with only a few shrubs. The barren landscape reminded Adam of a desert, even though it was atypical for Czechoslovakia. After two hours of a rough ride, noise, and dust, the truck stopped at a post with two other men in uniforms. Adam saw the guards laugh as the driver told them something funny and then the truck proceeded into the camp. The inner area was surrounded by a tall chain link fence with coiled barbed wire at the top. Several barracks lined a dusty dirt road and a large court with flag poles. More soldiers approached and ordered the recruits to get off the truck. They were ordered to create a row and stand silently, while a lower ranked officer read out names, yelling at the top of his lungs. The yelling was not necessary, but it was a sign of the military culture.

The names were read in a reverse order: last name first, followed by the first name. The correct answer was a loud "here." Adam figured his name would be called last. He was used to being the last in the alphabet. The last may become the first, he thought.

The officer read name after name, shouting loudly. Somewhere in the middle of the alphabet, he started distorting names into what sounded like comical cartoon characters. Gradually it got worse.

"Prince! Prince, Marek," yelled the officer, waiting for the answer that did not come.

He repeated the name and stepped up the pretense of anger. No answer.

"Perhaps you're looking for Marek Pintz," Marek called out in a calm voice.

"What? Pintz...Prince, you are not going to mock me!" yelled the officer, red in the face. "I'll show you what we'll do with you, you decadent piece of aristocratic shit!"

Marek was almost white in the face but he did not respond. It was the only thing he could do and they all knew it.

❧

In the next hours the boys became soldiers. First they got a violent buzz cut, their multicolored hair piling on the dirty concrete floor. Stripped naked, they had to hand over their clothes and possessions, each receiving a number in case they would live to see freedom again.

They passed along a row of tables stacked with green pants, shirts, underwear, and socks, each time signing on the bottom line of a list for the records. Dressed in the new garb, they followed a yellow line on the floor that led to the wooden barracks with endless rows of bunk beds and lockers, all green.

A new officer yelled orders on how to arrange and

organize their lockers. Surprisingly, they could choose a bunk buddy freely. Adam stayed with Marek and chose the top bunk. They were given short time limits for every task, without a chance to finish before the deadline. It was as if they had entered a different reality, a parallel universe where running and yelling was the norm. For dinner all they had was bad soup, stale bread, and a sour tasting pickle. By 22:00 they had to be in their bunk and the lights were out. The room was cold, and the sensation was multiplied by the recent loss of their hair. No one was sleeping. By 23:00 some of them were still whispering their impressions from the day. By 24:00 most soldiers were sleeping under the horsehair blankets.

At 5:30 the bell rang and the drill sergeants were screaming out in the corridors. Everything seemed to be back in high gear. Hastily, Adam got dressed in sweat pants and a tee shirt, as he was told to do. They ran out the door, onto the open courtyard. Morning exercise was obviously taken seriously. The instructor's voice was recorded, and amplified through scratchy loud speakers. The officer in charge of the exercise was observing the lazy ones with their sloppy, uncoordinated movements. He approached each of them in turn, ordering them to drop down and give him twenty push-ups. He achieved his goal of wiping the smirks off their faces. After thirty minutes of fresh air, the men were prompted to perform their daily hygiene like cattle.

The washrooms had several rows of long troughs, with a single drain at one end.

Rough plumbing delivered cold water at several locations. Adam found a place at the next available faucet and washed his face and underarms. So did Marek beside him. Soon a river of soap bubbles and toothpaste was flowing down the long gutter towards the drain. The last man stared at the pond of bubbles and spat before it ran down the slow drain. No one lingered; the water was just too cold. Back at the bunk, they changed into uniforms and ran to the line up in front of the barracks.

Three rows were formed and the men were ordered to turn right.

"March."

"Left. Left, right, left," yelled the officer in charge of the unit. The soldiers marched to the canteen.

Breakfast didn't seem like a bad idea. Personal aluminum dishes were among the hundred pieces of equipment they had received the day before. Three dishes fit into each other in a nesting position, the lid closed them together tightly, and a handle folded over the entire assemblage to lock it for transportation. Someone ought to get a design award for this dish set, Adam thought. The large dish was used for tea or soup. The tea was served from a huge pot, hot and smelly. The bad taste was created by the grease residue from dinner the night before. Bread and a can of spam were all they were served. Adam thought about Kirsten, of the times they shared breakfast. Hurry, hurry.

Everything happened quickly, and the aim was to keep the soldiers busy. In spite of their pace, Adam managed to keep a conversation going with his new friend Marek.

"Where do you live in Praha?" asked Adam.

"In the old town. We share a large flat with grandma."

"That's pretty good," decided Adam.

"Yes, but we have three children. We could use more space," said Marek. He spoke with a soft voice, placing emphasis on the key words which were hierarchically sorted by their information value. You could tell he was an intellectual to the bone. Furthermore, he knew people in Praha involved with arts and culture, and he was friends with many of them. Adam was similarly connected in Bratislava, so they found time for long conversations whenever they could steal a minute. After breakfast they were ordered to pack all their gear into duffle bags and line up for count.

"We want to welcome you by giving you the opportunity to experience the true beauty of military life," promised one of the drill sergeants. Surprised, the boys stared at a convoy of vehicles. The trucks started their diesel engines with a metallic roar and the drill sergeant invited the young men to jump up onto the bed. "What are you waiting for?" he yelled. "A first date?"

Once in the military, nothing is permanent. This includes function, position, equipment, and your next meal. Life becomes a rough river of circumstances, in which the raft floats rapidly from one rock to the next. A soldier has to be aware and avoid collisions with the rocks, whatever they might represent.

The trip was not too long. An hour and a half of dusty and noisy transport brought them to another set of scenery. This time they stopped at an old building north of Breclav with thick stone walls and small windows. In its better days, the structure used to be a medieval monastery. Now the building was almost a ruin, its purpose perverted into a military boot camp that was known for its harsh treatment of new recruits. The truck stopped in a courtyard and the silence made Adam feel dizzy.

The boys lined up and orders were barked at them by the "wise ones." "Wise ones" was Marek's nickname for the brainless senior officers so that he and Adam would be able to talk about them without being understood. They eventually developed a secret language that prevented an eavesdropping snitch from recognizing any names in their conversations.

One of the officers was a dark, gypsy looking sergeant with missing teeth and greasy hair. The shoulders of his uniform were covered with dandruff. It was obvious to Adam that these people were just an excuse for officers, a mere disgrace of military personnel. Even the military camp was a pathetic substitute for a camp. Later it became clear that the officers were assigned to this camp as a form of punishment, tied up there just like their subordinates. To Adam it only proved that everything was relative.

"You came here to forget all the crap you've learned at your stupid schools. This is your university now and we will teach you everything," yelled the officer. "We have methods for that."

Marek stood next to Adam, barely covering his amusement. Adam saw him, and they almost burst out laughing. As though the sergeant had heard them, he continued yelling. "If any one of you finds this funny, we will soon annihilate the humor in you!"

It became almost impossible to hide the laughter they kept inside. But laughing out loud would have been a suicide, and they both kept as still as they could.

The unit was ordered to run up the stairs to their new quarters and get organized for the day. An old, medieval structure, the building was made of stone and brick, with wooden floors that had seen better times. The rooms had high ceilings and small windows with iron bars embedded deep in the brick. Bunk beds crowded the rooms. The bad news was that there were forty men per room. The good news was that all of them were graduates and quite civilized, keeping the spirits up with their sense of humor.

The beds were not made, and their metal night stands had to be organized with their clothes folded and stacked per regulations. Any deviation from the standards was punishable. The men busied themselves folding shirts, pants, and making their beds. No one was a hundred percent sure they were doing it correctly because the instructions had been passed from room to room like a game of telephone. It could have been all wrong.

After an hour or so, the drill sergeant started his round, checking the quality of work.

Each man stood in front of his bunk, unsure of what was to come. Most of the beds and cabinets didn't pass the test. The sergeant yelled profanities and yanked the clothes out of their cabinets, scattering them on the floor. Kicking the clothes with his boot, the officer worked himself up to an agitated state, with a noticeably generous vein engorged on his neck and face.

"We might have a heart attack here," whispered Marek, giving Adam a jolt of reality. Adam tried not to smile.

The officer came to the bunk that Adam shared with Marek.

"Let's look at how a prince would make his bed," the sergeant said, trying to be funny. "His highness knows shit about making a bed!"

He ripped all the sheets and the blanket off the bed and threw them on the floor. He stepped on them as if performing his victory dance, yelling, "Doctor Pavlov taught a dog to salivate on cue, and we will teach a prince new tricks!"

After the sergeant left, the routine started over again. They folded shirts, socks, boxer shorts, and tank tops. All green, and all asking for mending. One guy whose older brother had served in the military a few years before suggested they use one centimeter wide strips of cardboard to mark the edge where the garments should be folded. That filler gave their shirts the straight edge crease that would pass the test of neatness.

This activity lasted till late in the day because there was no rush in the military. The mission was to keep the soldiers busy so that they would not have time to think about better pastimes. The purpose of the constant yelling was to keep the young men under high levels of stress in order to prevent free thinking. The intention was to break their spirits and their personalities. It was amusing for Adam and Marek to comment on such a transparent strategy. It worked on average brains, but some of them could not be so easily brainwashed. That's why the officers resorted to breaking them physically.

After an unmemorable dinner, most of the men tried to mend their clothes and gear.

A few others were on cleaning duty, scrubbing

toilets, floors, and making all the surfaces look wet. Two things were always welcome in military: fresh paint and wet mopping. Everyone learned quickly that whatever surface was visible, it was best if it was freshly painted or just mopped. For the soldiers the art of mopping meant the right balance of water without puddles. If the surface dried right after the mop passed, it was definitely too dry. Puddles were no good either. The zen of mopping got to be one of the soldiers' top favorites.

Any kind of reading had to be done between twenty-one hundred and twenty-two hundred. At 22:00 the lights went out and nighttime started. The men were tired, more mentally than physically. It became habitual to fall asleep three seconds after hitting the pillow. Marek and Adam talked every evening, comparing observations from the day, but even they didn't stay awake long. The building was not heated, so the room was filled with the smell of body odors and the chilly fall air.

By the second week everyone was getting used to the boot camp. The officers were determined to break the soldiers and make them subscribe to the system. The young men's responses varied from indifference to depression to wild rebellion. The rebellious ones were often punished by extra duties, frequently cleaning the toilets, washing the dishes, and spending nights in a secluded cell in the basement.

Rumors had it that an architectural school graduate who had spent several nights down in the holding cell in the filthy basement had figured out the puzzle of a missing corridor. As he was looking at the floor plan through the steel bars of his small cell, it dawned on him that one of the corridors dead ended illogically and did not match the floor plan above. He made a sketch and when he was released from isolation he and three other guys broke through the wall at the end of the hallway. They had to move a heavy storage cabinet first, and then remove a few bricks. Behind the brick wall they found a large room full of wine bottles. Vintage wine used to belong to the monks, who were now gone from official life in Czechoslovakia. They ceased to exist as an institution, and their wine now became the people's property. Regardless of its origins, nothing could have stopped the soldiers from drinking this found treasure.

An amazing drinking adventure became the new secret of the camp. Every night select soldiers snuck down to the basement and pushed away the large cabinet hiding the opening to the "cave of treasures". Backpacks were filled with bottles and tracks had to be covered. After the official bedtime, all paid officers had left for their homes in Brno and the graduates were literally locked in the building with only three guards on duty. The guards were selected from their own ranks and received a red or golden ribbon with a machine gun shell attached to one of the straps. These guards were supposed to stay up all night, reporting by telephone to the superiors, and keeping the other soldiers, who were given no weapons, under strict control. Their duties were usually taken seriously because any kind of problem or disobedience was punishable by serious jail time, but the guards agreed to be a part of the wine distribution. That made it possible for the wine adventure to go on for two weeks, undetected. Some witnesses later recalled that the hundred and sixty men drank almost a thousand bottles of wine during these amazingly strange times. The problem was that regardless of the severity of their hangovers, every morning the men had to wake up, exercise to the rhythms of propaganda songs, wash, and dress, all in a hurry. The ones who were slow, or had hard times with the drills, were punished in various unique and special ways.

One of the boot camp's special punishments was having the soldiers clean tile grout in the courtyard of the building. It was not the cleaning so much as it was the tools. The soldiers had to use their own tooth brushes, get on their knees, and scrub the endless grout lines of the thirty by forty yard court. Of course the tooth brushes were gone in the first hour. Then other tools were provided by the officers, who obviously enjoyed the role of the punishers. It was all a spectacle in the theater of the absurd.

Their month at boot camp was soon over and the men were transported back to Kramolin. By this time most of them were desperate for their girlfriends, wives, or any other female, regardless of how imaginary the thought was. This deprival of sex had a strange effect on the soldiers' behavior in the camp. Some became aggressive, while some just resorted to frequent masturbation at night. The group laughed at the sounds of heavy breathing and the vibration of the bunk beds, yet eventually no one was spared. If they hadn't done it consciously, it arrived through a dream.

Their new home was in the two-thousand-man facility close to Kramolin. It was to be an unforgettable experience of the Communist government's attempt to break down their intellectual opposition. The obvious targets were university graduates whose files gave them less than a clean bill of obedience, such as sons of dissidents, young priests (studies of theology were officially legal), boys with relatives who defected to the West, and other rebellious types like Adam, who corresponded with dozens of friends from all over the world. With time it became more and more clear that the secret police files on these young men were thick with reports on their activities and hobbies.

This facility had yet another purpose besides punishing the men. It had to do with the way this punishment was masterfully planned. The graduates were put in charge of other men, mostly petty criminals and gypsies, to make the men work physically every day of their time in the military. As it became clear within days, the assignment was to build a nuclear power plant very similar to the one in Chernobyl from Russian blueprints, this one near the southern border with Austria. The military provided cheap labor to the few civilian workers and engineers that were burdened by the same task.

The daily exercise routine was eliminated from day one. The officials had other ideas for physical fitness. Muscles were put to work. At 06:00 the amplifiers announced the new day, sparking a mad rush through hygiene and a line-up for the count. Then a fast march to breakfast where they were served mostly bread with the same distant cousin of spam, hard-boiled eggs, along with a fake coffee called "Kavona," so that at least the name was reminiscent of coffee. At 07:00 the troops were loaded into buses, with standing room only, and transported to their work. The one hundred and sixty or so graduates were superiors to the soldiers-workers, to keep an eye on their performance.

The result was as expected—the people in the lowest ranks started to hate their closest superiors, failing to see the broader picture. A class conflict of sorts. It was a perfect chance for the proletariat to fulfill the prophecy of Karl Marx: hatred of the intellectuals, who were otherwise known as the intelligentsia. This was a term created for the intellectual elite, who were mostly hated by Communist dictators like Lenin, Stalin, and their successors. In the early years of Soviet Russia, educated people were frequently imprisoned or killed, often with their entire families. Many intellectuals spent the rest of their lives in Gulag, a term for involuntary exile in remote places in Siberia.

Adam's new home was not a Gulag, yet the idea of a forced coexistence of general populace with intellectuals was an old recipe. Adam was in charge of thirty men, while Marek was simply placed in a unit as a worker. The officers were determined to teach "the prince" a lesson. At 07:45 they all punched in and picked up their tools. Tall towers marked number one, two, and three loomed high above the muddy construction site.

The forty-five minutes ride to the towers in a packed bus was torture. The men were packed in until there was standing room only. The worst was the smell of sweaty bodies, damp and dirty uniforms, and bad breath from rotting teeth. Most of the men ignored any kind of hygiene for weeks at a time, and their shaved heads made them all look alike. Their work uniforms were thick tan-colored denim overalls and a denim shirt, with another denim overcoat stuffed with old rags to keep warm. During winter temperatures reached twenty degrees Celsius below zero. A spit could fall on the ground frozen.

Adam had given his men instructions for the tasks of the day. They needed to prepare the forms for a concrete pour inside the reactor building. This involved preparation work such as digging, leveling, and hauling dirt in wheel barrels.

"Make sure nobody disappears from this area. I want to see you busy so this work will get done!" Adam called out.

"Yes, boss-general, we will fulfill this task at one hundred percent. We will make sure the imperialists will not catch us sleeping," Marek said. Adam knew that he was just quoting phrases from his favorite book *The Black Barons* by Svandrlik. It was a story about a similar labor camp with a practically identical scenario. The wry humor in the novel was very close to Marek's own. It was as if the situation had been staged straight from the novel.

"Hold your comments, soldier," Adam said playing along. "You will have plenty opportunities to prove your higher state of conscience and build this atomic power house for future happy generations."

It was quite warm inside the reactor building because they were sixty feet below ground. The lights illuminating the gigantic space underlined the fact that daylight was somewhere else. Everyone worked at a steady pace, just fast enough not to catch the attention of some civilian worker. A complaint from the "civils" could be damaging.

Adam experienced daily stress from having to force unqualified men to do work with marginal results. If the work was poor, which it almost always was, he could be punished by various methods developed by the officers in charge. Adam's unit was also quite bizarre in itself. Construction workers, a butcher, a locksmith, a Jesuit priest, several farmers, five potentially dangerous gypsies, and Marek made up their ragtag bunch. Still, everyone slowly found their groove. There was always the next day, and the next one after that. Some work did even progress in spite of their seemingly impossible scenario. Little by little, the power plant was growing. Adam wasn't sure if the unavoidable flaws caused by the unskilled and unsupervised labor would result in a catastrophe. Being behind schedule was a given, yet rumors circulated around the camp that the nuclear fuel rods had already been delivered by the Russians and they were stored next to the south fence of the construction site in a metal warehouse. No one wanted to go and check it out.

"What will this new and beautiful day on this deserted island bring to Robinson and Friday?" Marek often commented to Adam in the morning.

Adam was not sure who was supposed to be Friday and who got to be Robinson, but he also felt like someone stranded on a deserted island. There was some relief when Marek found a group of other soldiers very interested in reading. Mostly they were interested in books that were banned by the Communist regime for their inflammatory content. Books of this kind had to be hidden from plain sight. Mattresses were sliced on their sides and sewn together with quick stitches to contain books, magazines, and even pornography, as well as small illegal weapons such as knives and blades. Adam re-read some of the books despite the fact that most of the ones the soldiers passed around had already been circulated in his previous book club.

In addition to the books, Adam also looked forward to the mail. His family wrote many nice, long letters in small script that described the activities at home. They brought the excitement of having something to open that was private and personal. Letters were also a witness to distances, carriers, and places, holding smudge marks from dirty post offices and postal cars at the end of each train. Some letters had the scent of perfumes on them, and evidence of tears falling onto the ink, smudging the writing in places. Letters were touched by the hand of the authors, postal workers, receiving officers, and secret police screeners that had learned the skill of opening and closing the envelopes without trace.

Ironically, against all efforts from the government to isolate and brainwash the young men, letters were effective in preserving their relationships from home until the gates of the military camps opened to release the tired and broken individuals. The letters were distributed once a week, usually on Sunday, like a sermon and a message from god. The news from home was read over and over again before sleep, or during lunch when they gathered together. Soldiers carried the letters in their pockets in the original envelopes, as if they were an inherent part of the living organism, some sort of a shell that protected them from unauthorized reading.

Days became routine except when unexpected breakdowns came out of nowhere. Every once in a while some unfortunate guy lost his marbles and attacked another soldier. Sometimes the soldier just could not stand his situation anymore, and sometimes there was a real illness present. Of course there were some men who faked a mental illness to get discharged earlier.

No matter what the reason, these events were reminders that something insane had penetrated the lives of all the men in the camp.

Come December the temperatures dropped well below minus twenty. Soldiers felt the chill in their bones, so deep that the bitter cold felt as if it touched their souls within. The construction site was covered in ice and the mud was frozen into tire track sculptures. Adam thought of the Russian constructivist photographers with their abstract geometric shapes like Kandinsky paintings. Gigantic trucks carved the ruts into the landscape and the frost did the rest overnight. Small construction shacks were scattered around the enormous site among equally enormous cranes, transporters, and conveyors. Each of these shacks had a small wood-burning stove with a chimney piercing through the roof. White smoke rose from the stack, reminiscent of little dwellings for some nation of Hobbits who were building a colossal structure for an invisible wizard.

The soldiers had received fur hats with flaps covering their ears that tied under the chin with a string. Adam thought that the hats were Russian import from the Gulag. Scrap wood was chopped into pieces and fed into the fire. Pravda newspapers were the best starter and most of the soldiers thought it was the best use of the propaganda-filled daily papers anyway. Burned in a wood stove, they helped the survival of the proletariat, as intended by Karl Marx. Other good uses of the official printed ideology included stuffing Pravda inside shirts for better insulation.

Yet the final and best use was quite symbolic. It substituted as a toilet paper. The Communist leaders and the opportunistic dissidents alike used it for the same purpose.

Adam had just returned from his round at the construction site and slammed the door of one of the shacks. Inside there was heat and there was life. Outside, the temperature was eighteen below zero, and it felt like camp four on Mount Everest. Snow was driven by the wind as it blew through the open plain of the Mohelno desert. The immediate contact with the warm air inside felt painful as Adam's jaws, hands, and feet shook from the cold. Not even his green knitted mittens protected him against those temperatures.

The fresh snow had arrived and had been falling relentlessly for two weeks. Soon the only work possible under those conditions was inside the reactor building. With their slower schedule, the civilians often brought vodka to work and the men got drunk. Morals were in disarray. Adam was in charge and he was losing control. Every time someone got drunk the individual was thrown in a solitary isolation for twenty-four hours. Then Christmas came and everyone mellowed down. The strong atheistic ideology had no obvious impact on traditions. Party members and apparatchiks gladly put up Christmas trees and nativity scenes. If ideology and traditions were playing paper, rock, and scissors, ideology would be a rock, and traditions would be paper. Religion would be scissors. Or just a bigger rock.

During the holidays, Adam and Marek found ways to explore the possibility of enriching their cultural life. Some of the "civils" from the construction were willing to take them to Brno at the end of the shift. The unit had to report their presence every evening, but there were ways to have someone else report them on duty elsewhere. Of course it was risky and it could land them with jail time, but to the culture-hungry young men it was worth the risk. The timing was right, as everyone was busy with preparations for the holidays, and Brno had quite an interesting theater scene. Marek suggested they try to see Bolek Polivka's play, the *Jester and the Queen*. The civilian worker drove them practically to the entrance of the theater to avoid being confronted by the military police. They did not have a proper uniform used for leave. In fact, they hardly looked like regular soldiers because their unit was merely a labor camp in disguise.

The tickets were sold out, but in the old country anything was possible with a little conversation. In five minutes, the man at the box office promised them a special additional space and led them inside. Adam was never sure if theatre imitated life or life imitated theatre. The box office manager showed them a place on the carpet in front of the first row. The stage was only forty centimeters above the floor, so sitting on the carpet was actually like having the best seats in the house. Lucky, lucky, thought Adam.

Adam looked around the theatre. All the available additional chairs had been put to use, and people were standing in the aisles. Adam enjoyed the familiar pre-performance sounds of the audience. Then the lights went off and a small spot illuminated the beloved actor Bolek Polivka. The music sounded medieval and Bolek started to apply makeup to his face right there in front of people. He transformed himself into a jester. His queen, whom he served well for many years, was French and she did not speak Czech. "She does not speak Czech...," Bolek said loudly.

The actors spoke with dual meaning, in double thought, double-tongued sentences, mocking the corrupted Communist system. Humor was the weapon of mass "distraction". People needed to laugh, and the actor delivered that. The avant-garde approach was both a diversion and a cover-up. It was a statement and an escape. It was all and nothing. Sometimes it was a risk and sometimes it was an alibi. The society needed to vent the pressure cooker. People were ready to see exposed flesh. Bolek and his queen gave it to them in abundance.

The atmosphere in the theatre could not have been more in contrast with the last six months of the military camp. Adam and Marek, mesmerized by the art, were sitting on a carpet right under the stage and the main actors were addressing them as if a part of the script. At one point the queen called upon them, "Guards, come here and take him!" pointing to her jester. "They can't take me, they do not possess any weapons," the jester quipped back.

He was right, Adam thought. Their time served in

the military was just as fake as the society's need for their army. Instead of serving to protect their country, they kept busy with meaningless activities so that they would not rise above the mundane, aspire to grow and prosper. Freedom was denied to them because freedom was a drug, leading to addiction to a beautiful and fulfilling life. The performance was everything that Adam and Marek could have wished for. Their batteries were recharged, and their hearts were filled with new joy. It had such an effect on the young men that they didn't care what would happen if they were caught.

The tough part was getting back to the camp before dawn and slipping into the barracks without a big commotion. The only way was to hitch a ride in a truck making an early delivery to the camp. Two lucky rides later and the fugitives were safe again. Their luck held—the guards on duty were their buddies from Bratislava, so the re-entry went smoothly. It was four in the morning and their state of ecstasy was slowly receding.

*H*uman passion is like oil rising onto the surface of the water. Adam felt this the day he observed an old wooden structure behind the barracks. It was apparently a former outhouse, but it was obviously not being used for its original purpose. Upon examination, the outhouse stood firmly on the ground, minus a pit underneath. The seat had a hole and the doors were adorned by a cutout heart for ventilation. The outhouse must have been a relic from the times when the land belonged to farmers and village folks, before the military madness brought slave labor to the area.

It seemed like a good idea at the time to adapt the structure for a better use. Adam was missing his art studio and the intimacy of personal space. Generally speaking, there was no place to hide. Adam quickly got to work lining the inside walls of the abandoned outhouse with Pravda newspapers. The electric power was brought in via a pilfered extension cord from the construction. Adam hung a Kafkaesque light bulb from the ceiling, which cast a dim light on the Pravda wallpaper. Adam tested the light-proofing of his new art studio. With the doors properly closed, no light escaped to the outside.

The space was only three feet by four feet, but it was private and personal, reminding Adam of the freedom he left behind. And besides, the rent was cheap.

Adam started to draw and paint with the potency of a sailor returning after a long voyage. It was now eight months into his military service, a long eight months of imposed artistic silence. Adam began to express himself again, as though exposing layers of solidified mud. His paint supplies were borrowed from the propaganda closet, where they were normally used to paint Communist slogans. Charcoal came free from the stove after the ashes cooled. Canvases came from torn bed sheets, recycled before they were tossed into garbage. Paper was also available at the construction site. Adam felt alive again, painting deep into the night after the other soldiers were tucked in bed.

"Who are we tonight?" asked Marek. "Gauguin sailing the Pacific Ocean? Goya having bestial visions? Or perhaps Toulouse Lautrec visiting a brothel?"

"Just a hungry painter escaping the brutal conventions of the everyday life," Adam said. Marek was his only confidant and they both knew to keep mute about the outhouse space. They could not expect anyone else to understand the new fine art venue within the environment. Marek was the appreciative aficionado, the patron, and the benefactor all in one. Adam presented his new work at occasional late night studio visits, sharing his vision with the only friend who understood his calling.

First sketches were cumbersome and awkward, as if every movement of Adam's hand was discomfited by the eight months of artistic pause. Images slowly surfaced from the depth of the paper, initially with hesitation, then with the sure movement of a trained hand. Just like riding a bicycle, Adam's sense of balance did not vanish. Sketches became paintings and the surreal nature of the surroundings gradually soaked into the core of his bizarre artistic expression. The walls and ceiling of the outhouse were soon covered with paintings and drawings, transforming Adam's space into a universe of its own. Figures with ardent expressions froze in critical motion and spoke with soundless language. Landscapes expressed in hues of black, gray, burned umber, and tan pulled the viewer deep in its embrace, like emotions of a coal miner on a December day. A small opening of vivid color appeared in the background—inviting, seductive, and tempting. A tease of promise, or perhaps a glimpse of freedom. All in that tiny fleck of bright color in a field of gray mud. Hope. This gave Adam hope. His mind raced to imagine a world out beyond the barbed wire fence. In a world where words counted. Where ideas would prevail. A world where the expansion of his mind was limitless.

The works created in the old outhouse may have been inferior to Adam's customary daring and innovative art work, yet the mere existence of that channel felt like heaven to him. His fatigue was evident during the day however, when Adam often fell asleep momentarily and without warning. Officers yelled at him when he fell asleep over his lunch, and suspicion slowly set in. Adam did not paint every night, because it was physically impossible. On the nights that he did, Adam pretended to sleep first. The guards were on duty every night. They were soldiers like Adam, but it was not practical to disclose secrets to them. Sooner or later someone always squealed. Once the guards had settled down, the actual getting in and out of the small structure had to be done after dark.

Even with all the obstacles, Adam kept working on his new artwork within his strange confines. Perhaps creating art is similar in its psychological process to the needs of the physical body. Art is not merely documentation and a portrait of the world as seen by the naked eye. In fact, a true painter does not see with his eyes, but rather with the mind, a subconscious processor of intellectual food, some fresh and some stale, some fast and cheap, and occasionally a work of some culinary master.

Finally late fall arrived, and with it came the day when Adam's unique artistic freedom was taken away. Someone must have observed Adam going frequently to the mysterious outhouse. He did not keep any locks on the place, so checking it when he wasn't there was easy. It was a miracle it lasted so long. As if the perpetrator was acting in some bizarre drama, the officer that he reported to organized a sting operation. Instead of asking Adam to explain, the officer, major Kafarsky, prepared a surprise visit.

That night Adam was finishing his latest and last work before the winter would set its cold teeth into his flesh. Quietly, he placed brush strokes on a canvas as the doors opened violently. The construction lights, aimed at Adam, were practically blinding. His eyes could not adjust right away, but he heard a loud voice through a megaphone. Major Kafarsky was speaking as if he had just caught a criminal. They extracted Adam from his atelier and seized all his artwork, which amounted to twenty or so paintings and twice as many drawings. A few days later, after spending a night in the slammer, Adam was called to Kafarsky's office.

"So you are an artisto," charged Kafarsky. "What kind of sick idea is that, here in the era of imperialist danger lurking everywhere, that you dare to ignore the dangers and waist your time on some decadent activity?"

"Sorry, sir," declared Adam.

"If you were at least painting something worthy, like nude women, I would understand," Kafarsky said slyly.

"I am abstract," was the short answer from Adam.

"Is that some kind of disease?"

"No sir, it is just a type of expression in art," Adam said, trying to explain.

"I can have you imprisoned for at least six months."

"I was not doing anything against the system sir."

"You were undermining the task our proletarians are set to achieve! Who needs art anyway?"

Suddenly Adam realized that Major Kafarsky seemed to be enjoying himself. It was a joke to him, although he was not laughing. He was clearly acting for the benefit of appearing in charge of this momentous situation.

"I will have you whipped," tried Kafarsky. By this time he couldn't keep a straight face.

He was barely holding back his laughter.

"Where are my works sir?" asked Adam.

"I had them stored as future evidence," Kafarsky said. "And consider yourself lucky if I don't throw you to the lions."

The joke was out, but Adam knew better than trying to overstep the boundaries. "Thank you, sir," he said.

"Get out of here!" yelled Kafarsky, while he exhaled a huge plume of smoke from his cigar. He appeared to be imitating Stalin, Churchill, and Castro all at once.

As it turned out, Major Kafarsky was an eccentric himself, and if it hadn't been for communism, he would have been a comedian or a chef. Instead, Kafarsky became a new collector of Adam's art.

⁓

Not long after the episode of being caught in the outhouse, Adam was sent to a command headquarters in the regional capitol. At first, this seemed as an unexpected relief from working at the construction. Building the nuclear reactor with two thousand other men was hard work. It was either muddy or dusty, and sometimes too hot, other times too cold. But the reason for his new orders was rather devious. Adam was sent there to paint a mural of Vladimir Ilyich Lenin on the wall of the western command conference room. The reason he was given was that they wanted him to prove his new "credentials" as an artist. The catch was that the wall already featured a work of art. The building was another significant historic structure, dating into the 14th century. Originally it was a town hall, but it was later transformed into a monastery. The room selected for the new art project was a magnificent hall with cross vaults and pilasters around the perimeter. The walls were plastered and the largest wall featured a fresco with a battle scene of Saint George fighting a dragon that needed some serious restoration. Still, Adam could easily make out the horse, rider, spear, and the serpent's scales at the bottom under the horse's hoofs. The orders were to fix the wall with fresh plaster and paint a large portrait of Lenin over the mural. Adam thought this was either an evil joke from Major Kafarsky, or a case of ignorance and stupidity. Either way, it was his worst nightmare.

Adam soon realized it wasn't all bad. The first thing they did was place him in the monastery library to sleep. There were perhaps five thousand books there under the dust, just the way the Jesuit monks had left them when the Soviet military and the Czechoslovakian Army took over the building. Adam thought he had arrived in heaven. At night, after the resident soldiers went to sleep, he carefully looked at book after book, slowly realizing the proportion of this treasure. Some books were even created before the time of Guttenberg. Each page of those books had a hand painted image of astonishing quality followed by writing in an unfamiliar language. Some of the books were bound in leather, others were first editions, and many were just great works of literature. Adam was sure no one besides him cared about the value of this abandoned collection.

On the third day of Adam's stay at headquarters, General Petik called Adam to have a conversation about the artistic commission.

"Your commander Major Kafarsky said you were an artist. Is that accurate?" asked the general.

"That's accurate sir," Adam said as officially as he could.

"Art is decadent and proletarians do not need art. Do you know that, soldier?" barked the general.

"But we have very famous artists in our country sir."

"Can you imagine a farmer staring at some picture

after he spent his productive day preparing food for the common good? Some day we will send all artists away from this country to rot in capitalist hell."

"That is a good idea sir," Adam agreed. He didn't have to pretend this time. In fact, he would have liked to have been kicked out by the general.

"You have a very honorable task in front of you soldier so don't screw it up. You will paint a big head of Comrade Lenin on this wall." The general pointed to the wall with the precious fresco. "Make sure it will show him as the leader that knew everything. He has to look like he predicted the great future for all comrades."

"It will be my honor to do that, Comrade General, but I worry about that wall. It is already rotting, and if I put the face of Comrade Lenin on it, soon it will look like Comrade Lenin has a skin problem," Adam lied. He felt as if Marek's sarcasm had rubbed off on him and helped him put on this face of seriousness.

"I have a suggestion sir," offered Adam after a moment. "What if I prepare a quality canvas for this task, so that Comrade Lenin will not suffer on that wall?"

"Not such a bad idea, even if it is coming from an artist like you. I approve," the general said.

And so it was. A large canvas was stretched onto custom stretching bars, slowly and precisely. Adam worked as slowly as he could without anyone noticing, so that he could extend his vacation from construction. He looked at several artists for style and settled on making Lenin look like he was painted by Aleksandr Rodchenko, the popular propaganda artist of the twenties. Lenin must have known him in person, so the link seemed appropriate. Adam imagined that they drank together in a Bolshevik bar, surrounded by comrade women. His first idea was to model the portrait on the work of Egon Schiele, or Ludwig Kirchner, but he realized that the general would deem the work degenerate just like the Nazis did.

The day of the opening came and the general prepared a speech. Invited guests gathered, including another general, a few colonels, and some comrade women. The side tables were loaded with vodka. Lenin was unveiled, and there was applause. The work was quite mediocre. There was no point or desire for Adam to excel. Nothing mattered anymore. Adam had gone into a survival mode, knowing that if he woke up just one hundred more times, he would be going home. Everyone got drunk and sang predictable Russian songs. Some Russian songs can be beautiful, but these were not. The officers got into a discussion about the war, swapping stories about fighting the Nazis and how the Russians had prevailed at Leningrad. By midnight, Adam was their brother, and they all laughed about how the military was bullshit. That was pretty much the last thing Adam remembered before he passed out under the table.

The art gig lasted an entire month. Well fed, read, and rested, Adam returned to the everyday grind. But now his time in the camp was headed towards a countdown. The closer he came to the end, the wider the gap between him and his life back at home seemed to be. More and more Adam caught himself thinking about Kirsten, dreaming about the time they spent together in the snow covered Berlin, and creating new scenarios after the reel of their life went blank.

To kill time, the soldiers were working hard at creating their "Meters". These amazing calendars were made with a tailor's measuring tape, and were created one hundred and fifty days before the end of the military service. The number of days was not arbitrary, because the measuring tape was exactly one hundred and fifty centimeters long. The soldiers stripped the top layer of the tape to expose the canvas base. Then colorful imagery and writing was conceived, each centimeter representing another day. Such a labor intensive process was possible only in conditions of isolation.

The results were stunning. The "Meter" was then carried in the front pocket of its creator's uniform. At the end of every day, one centimeter piece was ceremonially cut off with scissors, as the soldiers celebrated the joy and anticipation of their release and return home. This tradition had a strange twist. The small, cut off piece of tape that represented a day in the camp, was then given to a new young soldier who had some seven hundred plus days in front of him. It was an act of subtle cruelty, and bragging rights to show off a very short "Meter" was common among the units. The shorter the tape, the more respect was given to its owner. An intense seniority principal was often connected to abuse and hazing among the soldiers. Adam and most other graduates did not participate in the hazing, but everyone had created a "Meter" for himself, including the intellectuals. It was just too hard to resist.

One morning a new situation arose. Major Kafarsky called Adam into his office and gave him orders to escort a prisoner to a remote jail in eastern Slovakia. It was a task both strenuous and dangerous, and the prisoner had to be handcuffed to his escort in order to be transported by train to the designated prison.

Adam immediately saw the possibilities. The route to the prison went through Bratislava, where he could see his family on his way back from eastern Slovakia. The key was to manage the prisoner safely. Often enough, an escort was found beat up somewhere in a ditch, and the jailbird at large. In this case, the inmate was a big fellow from western Czech named Slava Graber. He was actually from Sudettenland, the infamous area where Czech Germans lived happily before the war. Slava's name was also German, even though most Germans were expelled in exile in 1945. His height –six feet and eight inches—combined with three hundred pounds of muscle was frightening enough.

Adam was half the size of Slava. Cuffed wrist to wrist, they were like a planet and its moon. With relief, Adam quickly realized that Slava was one of the more mellow giants, smiley and pleasant most of the time. Occasionally, Slava admitted to having lost his temper, which made him crush someone's face like a meatball. His profession back in the west Czech was to stun cattle before butchering. The cows slowly walked the corridor of death, while Slava Graber stood above with a sledge hammer in his huge hands, delivering a lethal blow on the forehead of the poor animals. Even before the labor camp Slava spent some time in the slammer, mostly for drunk driving and alcohol-related violence.

The escort started with the official handcuffing. The irony was that the key was then given to Adam, who was to keep it in his pocket during their journey. The orders were given and the trip started. The truck brought them to the train station and left. Adam asked Slava if he wanted a beer. It was six in the morning, and Adam knew that the pub at the train station would open at seven.

Adam's initial plan was to take the train to Brno and switch trains. An express train to Kosice, then a bus ride to the county jail. A long trip with a strict set of rules. Adam could only un-cuff Slava while the train was in motion, during a bathroom break, or occasionally, when eating lunch. Even with the rules, Adam decided to interrupt the journey in Bratislava and spend the night at his family's home. Slava was fine with the plan, especially after Adam's promise of a limitless supply of beer and food. Under normal circumstances, this plan would have been considered insane. But life just wasn't normal those days, and Slava was enthused about arriving to jail a day late. He giggled and joked about Adam being arrested to serve the sentence with him. But the plan seemed ingenious at the time. The two escapees created a pact of cooperation. They were allies of convenience, like the tickbird and the zebra.

Bratislava greeted them with dust and heat. The agreement between the strange fellows was that they would travel without the handcuffs so they looked just like any two soldiers on leave. The danger was near and real. The military police could card them anytime. Adam had to think of how to get far away from the railway station, where the odds of being caught were high. Even though he worried, once they were on a street car, no one bothered them.

Bratislava looked prettier than ever. The sun was touching the cornices of buildings, lighting up layers of paint that could be peeled off to reveal lost centuries. The street car reluctantly glided over the rails, screeching around the curves of the road. People were on their way to work or school, and no one else was escorting a prisoner. Adam was tired, but he was staring at the familiar streets and storefronts of his home. Nothing had changed during the year. Slava was happy, observing the pretty women and commenting on their body parts under his breath. It took fourteen stops before they came to the neighborhood of Adam's parents. Slava was motivated to stick around, with a vision of beer and homemade food.

Adam's parents were warned about the visit when Adam called from a payphone at the railway station. Still, when he stood in front of the door, emotions came rushing in. Adam's mom estimated the damage done to Adam over his year away. He was twenty pounds lighter than before the camp. He was also sporting a huge mustache, partly to look like someone else during his time in the military, and partly to express seniority in the rankings. Young blood in the camp was not allowed to have any facial hair.

They ate lunch and dessert, and drank beer and more beer. Slava downed four beers, Adam two, and they figured out the program for the day. They thought the best thing was to go to the orchard and spend the day outside. Adam changed into his civilian clothes and Slava was able to fit into Adam's old sweat pants, and an extra large tee shirt. Even in disguise, they looked strange because of Slava's hulking figure. People stared at them as they made their way into the street car with Adam's family.

It was one of those slow, lazy, crackling hot summer days. The heat shimmered above the asphalt roadways, and the flies were buzzing in the heavy air. The two soldiers took a long nap in the shade of an apricot tree. Cold water from the well tasted like champagne. Everyone talked excitedly, sharing news of friends and family, many of whom came to see Adam during the day. Other family members came and brought food, like there was no tomorrow.

There was a tomorrow, but first there was the night in front of them. Slava was a complete stranger and he was supposed to stay overnight. Adam thought the best plan was to drink beer until Slava fell asleep. A case of Pilsner was placed in the fridge, chilled to the right temperature. That evening Slava drank fourteen beers and Adam six. They were both drunk. Slava resisted sleep by joking, singing, and talking nonsense about wanting to go out to a pub. That would have been the end. Adam was quite sure that if they went Slava would only have started a fight. Finally, Slava was yawning, and then he was asleep, stretched on the kitchen bench. Adam took a shower and went to bed.

A few moments later, Slava woke up in total darkness feeling hungry. First, he looked for the bathroom, banging into everything that was in his way. In a small apartment, in the middle of the night, all his sounds were amplified. He made his way into the kitchen, and opened up the fridge. Pots and pans were pulled out, and he started to eat. Two gallons of lentil soup made it down into the abyss of Slava's stomach. Meat, potatoes, cabbage, and all the other leftovers, chased by more beer, disappeared during this feeding break. He felt hot, so he tried to open the kitchen window that had been painted shut for years. He succeeded, although he ripped out the window handle, and settled down on a chair. In a few moments, he was fast asleep again.

During this interlude, no one but Adam could sleep. His parents were petrified from the simple presence of a bona fide criminal and hesitated to wake Adam, even if he could hardly prevent Slava's escape. The morning arrived, and Slava woke up again, with a headache and a request for scrambled eggs. He downed six eggs and a half loaf of bread, while Adam said goodbye to everyone. There were more tears and more affirmations about a safe and fast return, and Adam's mother handed them baked pastries in a brown bag. They were ready to go again.

By midmorning the escort and the prisoner were on the train to Kosice, and then the bus to the county jail. All seemed to be well. Nobody wondered where they were, it was just expected that people got to places when they got there. If they did not arrive, then there was the possibility of a problem, but nothing was immediate. The wheels of destiny rolled with ease and grace. Justice, happiness, pleasure, and all the rest of the world's tricks arrived slowly, yet surely. People were not in a hurry for the impossible. Things just happened.

Eventually Slava was delivered to the jail. The orders

showed that they were a day late. Adam gave some weak explanation about a missed train, but no one cared. The success resided in their mere arrival. The prisoner did not escape. No one was harmed. Adam was sent back to his unit.

*A*dam's time in the camp was ticking away, slowly, but surely. August was lazy like an overfed dog. No one paid attention to the troops. Seniority set in and the officers did not bother the senior soldiers beyond the obvious line of duty. Adam, Marek, and the other graduates were just killing time, reading books, and pretending some activity at work. The real work was now done by the newcomers.

"God help us if this nuclear power plant really works. The sloppy thing will probably blow up in the face of the Communist leadership," joked Marek one evening. He had no idea how close to the truth he was. Less than two years later, the catastrophe in Chernobyl changed the face of Ukraine. It was a similar power plant, with comparable technology.

Everyone was aware of the nuclear fuel rods, stored at the far end of the plant. These had arrived early, not anticipating delays in construction. An arbitrary buffer was set around this radioactive and potentially lethal storage. Adam avoided that end of the construction site, imagining Marie Currie glowing at night like a skeleton x-ray. Not a pretty picture. No one wore radiation detectors. No one checked when Adam ventured on trips outside the perimeter of the site, exploring farther corners of the Mohelno Desert. The big sky was picturesque, reminding him of paintings by the French Plen Aire painters. Yet Adam often looked at the ground while he walked, hoping to find some of the famous tear-shaped glass pieces left from the meteorite that had created the desert. In one direction, he could reach the edge of the desert with an hour's brisk walk. Beyond the barren wasteland, an agricultural area spread over several kilometers.

Walking away felt good. Perhaps complete escape would feel like that. Adam's mind escaped every day, running away from captivity like a dog let off his leash. Freedom of the mind proved superior to the freedom of the body. In nature, air, dust, wind, or rain touch our skin most notably when the layers of civilization are stripped off, connecting the rudimentary to the ancient. The sum of all the elements combined with Adam's physical body resulted in a feeling of total freedom.

At the edge of the desert, Adam walked for a half hour through a sea of green where the government had seeded enormous fields of corn, wheat, and barley. When the cooling towers of the nuclear plant were small bumps on the horizon, Adam realized that he was walking through a pea field. As far as the eye could reach, not a soul was in sight. Adam tried to eat the snap peas. They were sweet, so he kept eating them until he felt no hunger. The sun was relentless. He stopped and took off his shirt. The sun felt hot and suddenly he had an urge to strip off his clothes and expose himself to the wind and the heat. He carefully placed his clothes on the ground and rested his naked body on them. He was lost in the middle of vast acres of green, like a lone swimmer in the ocean, like a Bedouin in the Sahara, burning and thirsty. The sky was now a complete image, filling the peripheral reaches of his vision, allowing for no more than dreams. He imagined looking down from above and seeing his solitary and unprotected body.

Adam was in this trance until he felt his skin burning. He snapped out of this surreal world and reluctantly put his green shirt and pants back on again. Suddenly, he had a premonition. He was standing on top of a mountain in the middle of an island, with nothing but water around it. Maybe the image was invoked by resting his eyes on the infinite fields of peas, yet it felt so real. The place surrendered itself to his imagination, engaging all his senses in the interlude.

Adam walked for two hours before he reached the construction site, climbed the fence, and blended in with the rest of the unit just in time for the transport back to the barracks. He was physically present but his mind felt fully liberated, independent and sovereign in his command over the future. In this state he conceived a marvelous future, full of brave journeys and provocative art work. He shared his vision with Marek, who was sympathetic in his own way. They ate together, and promised each other a friendship beyond the camp, beyond the propaganda, and far into a new world after communism. Marek trusted Christ to deliver this eternal bliss, while Adam saw Christ in Marek, and all the people around them. It felt good at that time, and a fragment of that condition was to stay with Adam for the rest of his life, like a lucky companion on the road to nothingness.

"Nothing is everything," he thought, as he saw clearly

what he would change in his life after he was set free.

Summer was finally over and so was Adam's military service. He handed over his green clothes in exchange for his old civilian garb, and then the gates closed behind the soldiers. The chapter was completed, and history turned to a clean page. Good-byes were exchanged in haste. Adam told Marek he would visit him in Prague. Then they parted in different directions. It was over. The train ride home was mostly silent. Nearly all the men were immersed in their deep thoughts. Adam opened the corridor window and turned his face into the stream of air outside. He got a whiff of the smog from the diesel engine mixed with the first scent of autumn. The wind in his hair was refreshing, almost purifying. Freedom felt instantaneous as the train arrived to the cities and villages of their origin.

Adam was back in Bratislava, starting over again.

Starting over was strange but not as hard as Adam had thought it would be. The first week after his arrival, he had to do a good deal of partying and drinking with buddies around town. The river of beer and wine flowed through fields of conversations rich in philosophy, history, and current events as Adam's closest friends briefed him on a year of all the things he missed out on. A year that was suspended in time. It was time to wipe the slate clean. There was a sense of resurrection around him, the true meaning of leaving the old behind. What immediately confronted Adam was just how he would create his new existence.

In a world where there was a shortage of everything, not surprisingly, there was also a shortage of apartments.

However enjoyable his life as a bachelor was, his family's small apartment just didn't cut it. Now he needed a place of his own, a sense of privacy, in spite of the kindness and accommodating spirit within his family. He kept looking for the needle in a haystack.

Accepting those impediments was exactly what the Communist principles suggested. Adam reminded himself of the mantra, which suggested that everything belonged to everyone, and in a convoluted way, nothing belonged to anyone. But knowing that Marx and Lenin invented tools to enslave the poor majority of people, and then killed the rest of the population, was of no consolation. The lies people had to swallow seemed to be in endless supply.

It was not easy to come to terms with a prospect of life without options. No matter how anyone tried, there was no reward for hard work. Various restrictions were in place just in case someone had an enthusiasm for achieving more than his profile had granted. The majority of children were profiled during school years in order to create a file for their surveillance, and in this file most possibilities were summarized and capped, just as if they were breeding animals. Some had an allowance for an engineer, while others were slated to become doctors, and most were restricted to manual labor. The Communist party had to approve any and all advances. Career was a function of some bizarre pedigree which they determined. To Adam, living with this kind of prescribed plan seemed ridiculous and repulsive.

Chopin's *Waltz in a Minor* was escaping from the

127

windows of the local art school as Adam walked from the bus stop. He was often amazed that the people had not lost their appetite for learning music, dance or fine art, in spite of the dreary existence. Like a silent resistance, or a gentle revenge, a few cultural individuals indulged in the world of beauty. Culture had never died. Not even the worst period of Stalinism had extinguished the infatuation people had with beauty. Art is immortal, though sometimes suppressed and dormant in its embryonic stage.

Adam walked from the bus stop with Chopin in the background. By the time he reached the art school, the Waltz changed into *Ballade in g Minor*. The melody was so lovely that he sat down on a bench in front of the school and listened. With every note and harmony, he felt like an epiphany came down upon him. He saw clearly his life beyond the barbed wire. Of course he imagined escape before, may be a thousand times over. But now he saw it. Like a déjà vu, the Technicolor dream seemed almost real. He saw himself living elsewhere, and this image was so seductive that he almost choked with emotions. Suddenly, it was all clear. Adam felt emerged in the crescendo of music. He knew he would not waste any more time, and he would focus all his efforts on getting out. In that single minute all was lost and all was found. Whoever was playing the ballade on the piano that afternoon was part angel and part rascal, with almost full responsibility for the journey Adam would embark on. The scent of freedom, the love of his life, had never faded away. His happiness was a shooting star, much like a comet without destination.

The next day, full of energy, Adam entered an architectural competition for a new design of the regional theater and opera. He gathered a team and they started to work. He and his team also entered another competition for the design of a theater in Tokyo. It was very popular in those days to participate in the international competitions. Many architects were trying to show that design had no boundaries. The point was to design a great piece of architecture with all the logic and design parameters, like a probe into the freedom of expression. Routinely, teams from the Eastern Bloc succeeded in winning one of the main prizes, creating a problem for the Communist authorities because it was expected that the winners would pick up their winnings in person.

Adam and his team worked day and night on the designs. Schematic designs were discussed and argued with the aid of caffeine and adrenaline until the best solution was born. Buildings of national importance and prestige solidified on paper until the group's latest masterpiece was finished, or until the deadline came and no wine was left to be consumed.

When they had finally finished the theatre project, Adam sent out the finished plans to Japan. It was all anonymous, juried only by numbers assigned to each team. The weeks after they mailed out the design were painful in expectations. The team that scored the highest would win a great domestic and international acclaim. All architects in the community would talk about the design and celebrate the winners. Such were the times. Adam and his team must have been doing something right because they won several of these attempts. Never a first prize, but the second or third prizes were often awarded to his team. Unexpectedly, money was pouring in, enough to spend loads of it with friends and the team. With the rest of it Adam bought a brand new Fiat.

Driving an Italian car, albeit a small one, was an enormous distinction. Adam was gaining reputation as an architect and his social circuit was getting a little out of hands. Because of a failed system, he was still not allowed to leave the country to retrieve his winnings from the competitions. The check had to be mailed to him. He and most other people were stuck like caged chicken, even with improved personal economies. But a dawn of a new promise was on the distant horizon. To the east, the Soviets elected a new guy by the name Gorbachev. The perestroika had started.

The first thing that was noticeable during the perestroika reforms was a loosening of the business laws legalizing independent enterprises. For the first time small private businesses started to pop up. The political climate was also changing rapidly. The death grip that the Soviet empire used to have on the Eastern European countries was beginning to relax. People started to think as entrepreneurs and Adam, too, had devised a plan. He wrote a long letter to the University of Hawaii inquiring about a possibility of teaching at the architectural school there. The School of Architecture at the University of Hawaii was not too big, and it had a good architectural program. There was a focus on sustainable design and Polynesian structures, and the school was known for decent residential and urban design studios. Indeed, the school was looking for someone with a specialized focus on European architectural styles. They were even willing to file a petition for a special visa for visiting lecturers.

Adam filed an application, loaded with information about his credentials and achievements. Luckily, the school was interested, so the petition was filed for a temporary twelve month visa, and the impossible train had left the station. Adam had to deal with the same people who routinely threw obstacles in his way to bar him from travel. But the times were unavoidably changing. Old ways were more and more criticized by those brave journalists, who saw the potential for freedom supported by the perestroika. Perhaps the intelligent part of the population sensed the beginning of the end, or perhaps the bells were about to toll. After three years of turning every stone, the impossible happened. Adam got an initial approval for an academic foreign exchange trip. He was told he could go.

This was a point of no return in Adam's mind. Calling his buddy Marek in Prague, Adam confessed that this meant more to him than he had ever thought. Leaving was, suddenly, the only way, and it represented the critical mass of his disappointments. He had an itch to travel far and then a little further. Hawaii fit the bill because it was practically on the opposite side of the globe. Now he only needed the coveted American visa. Ironically, the red tape surfaced here, too, and the State Department lingered far behind schedule.

Finally the impossible happened and Adam was called to retrieve his visa from the American Embassy. A large stamp was affixed to the entire page in his passport. It smelled like heaven. He kept everything low-key but inside, his mind was racing and he couldn't sleep at night. He was trying to resist the feeling of ecstasy, since several trips were barred by local authorities in the past. A few days later his airline tickets arrived and it felt like a miracle. Adam was ready to leave right away, but the date on the ticket wasn't until June. Good-byes were huge. He saw family and friends, and everyone thought he might never return to his country again. In that political environment, no one would come back if they could help it. The broken system was like a dying horse. No one could imagine that the Berlin Wall would come down with a bang, or that the Communist regime would crack and evaporate in fumes, giving way to a more organized beast of a free market economy.

Adam's dinners and parties had no end. Then the time came to pack several suitcases and get a bus to the Vienna airport. Adam could not believe that his journey wasn't stopped right at the border. After the passport check and customs, he turned back to see Bratislava shrinking on the horizon like a pretty post card. He told himself he was out, outside the country, on the other side of the barbed wire fence. He was on his way to the heavenly place of his dreams. Was this freedom? The freedom he was dreaming about?

For now Adam only had a smile posted on his face, part foolish and part sad, as the sun peeked from behind the morning clouds. Where was Kirsten now? he wondered. A strange idea entered his mind. He imagined switching planes to West Berlin, where he would look for her, like a private detective. It was completely unrealistic because he did not even have a visa to Germany. He snapped out of this daydream and he refocused his mind on Vienna airport.

Part Four
Crossing the Ocean
1988-1993

11

The trip over the Atlantic was an all new experience for Adam. He entered a state of observant alertness, a skill he had learned by being exposed to new situations. An addictive overload for the senses brings out the best in human beings—the ability for learning and adjusting. We all have this capacity in our DNA, perhaps from the cradle of civilization, or maybe even prior to that. This proficiency to react and guard oneself in a new environment is only paralleled by walking through a dark forest, or an urban jungle. The survival of the fittest is actually the survival of the most vigilant.

The airport in Vienna was, as it is typical for airports, not exactly in Vienna. Even though it was small, the cafes and duty free shops were colorful and expensive. Adam noticed the price tags on goods offered at the colorful boutiques. He would have to use up all his cash for just one garment or a watch. This gave him a pause, thinking about life in the West, and the possibility for survival in an unknown economy. Suddenly he realized it was time to board his plane. After he handed over the boarding pass, he followed the path to the belly of the beast. A modern, biblical whale that would give him a ride to the New World.

The flight attendants were smiling as if they knew him well. The experience during the take off was priceless. The roar of the engines just before the departure symbolized the brutal separation from the placenta he left behind. The umbilical cord was now cut. It was easy to realize that no one could force him to come back now if he decided to stay. An hour into the flight his thoughts meandered back to Kirsten. Was she already living her dream? Was she happy, and had she made the right choice? The sky over the Atlantic was painted in shades of blue and gray. Slowly his thoughts were changing territory as he drifted to sleep. A microcosmic environment of three airports and 27 hours later, he surfaced in the tropical paradise.

The very first thing that hit Adam when he got out of the airport hall was the intoxicating fragrance of plumeria flowers. Delivered with an astounding wave of warm air, he knew immediately that the fragrance would never leave his mind. Once it entered the brain it created a new file in the mind that screamed Hawaii. Adam had expected some unusual physical sensations because he was pre-conditioned for surprises, but the real deal exceeded all of his expectations and it felt heavenly. The hot island breeze seduced Adam like a French mistress, claiming his heart forever as a trophy. And that was only his first minute on the sacred islands. The match was decided without a fight.

Everything seemed different, starting with the light. The light was incredible. Inanimate objects were dancing in a strange vibration, offering high resolution images. Adam just kept staring. A man from the university held a sign with Adam's name on it and introduced himself as Dr. Jim Brennan when Adam approached.

"But you can just call me Jim," he told Adam with a cheerful wink. Jim led them to his BMW parked outside, and slid Adam's suitcase inside the trunk. The dream continued as the car left the airport. The freeway opened up the view of the high, green mountains on the Mauka side. The Makai side presented a glimpse of the ocean, turquoise and entirely kitschy. Like a tourist postcard Adam had never believed to be authentic.

The car was humming along with open windows. The true islanders loved the breeze rushing through the interior, messing with their hair, reminding them that this was real, and that they were alive in this paradise on Earth. A few minutes later, they were riding along the beach and Adam wanted to scream. He opened his mouth as if he would shout, but the words were stuck somewhere deep in his throat, squeezed by emotions of bliss and ecstasy. Kalakaua Avenue obscured his view of the ocean for a minute, replacing it with a crowd of aloha shirts, colorful shops, and restaurants. Then the grand finale arrived with the open landscape of Kapiolani Park, with a golden beach on its right and Diamond Head to its left. Finally Jim made a sharp turn into a driveway, pulling into a parking garage of a private club.

"Welcome to Hawaii," pronounced Jim as he led Adam to a table where a woman sat. "This is my wife Kelly and I thought we might have a drink here before heading home. You'll be staying with us of course, and we want to make sure you have all the best first impressions."

137

Adam shook Kelly's hand in a daze and sat down. The moment was thrilling, Hawaii was charged with the power to make a believer out of a sinner, etching some kind of a divine symbol into the pulsating matter of the subconscious. Suddenly Adam felt a déjà vu stronger than ever before. He knew this was the place he had seen in his dreams. This was the place he saw when he stared into a dark ceiling during sleepless nights at the labor camp, when he had stretched himself out in an ocean of green crops. This happened to be the same ocean he was describing to his only friend Marek, while bitterly cold in the open planes of Mohelno Desert.

Now standing in front of his Technicolor dream he felt instantly at home. People who have experienced a déjà vu know that it is not just an invoked memory or some kind of pseudo-visualization. A real déjà vu is a fulfillment of some divine plan. It is not a replica of a memory, it *is* the memory. The waves were hitting the wall below their chairs in seven second intervals. A large wave splashed against the wall and the spray covered their faces. The air was filled with salt and seaweed, while the nearby sandy beach spread out under the flickering shade of tall coconut palm trees.

A beautiful Polynesian waitress delivered a pineapple juice with a large slice of the fruit sticking out of the glass. "Oh my God, pinch me," said Adam in a quiet voice. Jim smiled, remembering his own first encounter with the islands twenty-eight years ago. He told Adam how Kelly had talked him into moving to Hawaii after they were married and they had their first two children. By the time she was pregnant again he had agreed and their twins, Jackie and Josie, were born in Honolulu. All of their children went to Punahou high school where they all did well. "Hawaii is not just a place, it is a lifestyle," Kelly said with a laugh.

After a few drinks they decided to drive home so that Adam could wash up, rest and see where he would live for the year. The car raced swiftly up the Manoa Valley Road and wove its way through narrow residential streets near the University of Hawaii. The mountains up in the valley seemed to be covered with mist and rain. The last stretch of the road was steep, lined with more plumerias. Finally, they were on top of the hill. When Adam got out, his jaw dropped as he saw the view below them. He could see the lower Manoa Valley, Ala Wai, and all the way inside Diamond Head crater. Beyond that there was the blue ocean stretching as far as the eye could see. It took a while to process all this beauty. The view felt almost material—so real that it could sustain human passion for years.

The house was a humble, shingle style bungalow with Chinese roof edge, the rafters raised up in a slight curve. Kelly showed Adam downstairs to his room, which had a door leading straight out to the side yard. One double hung window let in the fragrance of plumeria flowers. The bug screen kept the occasional roach and centipede outside. In the space leading to the exterior door, there was a sink, toilet, and a small shower with a concrete floor and a shower curtain. It was like a miniature suite. Adam felt tired with jet lag. He took a shower and fell asleep. The dreams he had were perplexing and seemingly irrelevant to his recent experiences. In them he felt completely free of feelings. Only a pure sense of being without obligations, responsibilities, or commitments. He felt nothing, and he realized that freedom couldn't be felt or understood without being deprived of it. Without oppression, he could easily lose the distinction of freedom. Typically, we don't recognize light without knowing the darkness, and we don't know pleasure without knowing pain.

Adam woke up very early. The jet lag caused him to get up at five in the morning. Without a plan, he decided to explore the neighborhood. He loved discovering things without a map or a manual, learning from pure experience, as instinctive as a wild animal. He was known to find happiness in the thrilling rush of adrenaline whenever he tried new things. The morning air felt balmy, but not exactly warm as he walked. The plumeria trees were still there, loaded with flowers. Across the street, strange big flowers occupied the rock wall on the back side of Punahou High School. It was the Night Blooming Sirius, shockingly beautiful, almost to a point of signaling danger. They bloom only at night, displaying their size and beauty.

Adam walked without any specific purpose, just to get a feeling for the place he would live in for several months. It was relaxing to walk without a destination, looking at everything with a new pair of eyes. The abounding vegetation was unfamiliar to the newcomer. His attention spiked at the site of a mongoose, a weasel-shaped animal quick on its feet. There was silence everywhere, too early for the university students who habitually slept till midmorning. Even the coffee shop was not opened yet, although someone was baking scones behind the window. Adam felt a sharp desire to do something creative. He missed painting, creating artwork for fun or for exhibitions, where his art would be judged, critiqued, analyzed. He missed presenting his thought process to a crowd and having discussions and philosophical arguments with good friends. Stevo and Marek surfaced in Adam's mind. He remembered the good times talking and painting with them. It was essential to find an art studio fast. He couldn't hold all the new art ideas inside anymore.

He found his way back to the house and took a shower. Then he went upstairs to the kitchen to find something to eat. He ran into Kelly, who was an extremely early riser.

"Want some eggs? I made tea and toast, already".

"Sure, thanks."

"You can always help yourself to anything. There is cereal and milk most of the time." Kelly busied herself at the sink. "Where did you go so early?" she asked. "Jim is leaving for the office, and you are expected at the university at ten so when you're ready I'll drive you over."

The campus was very unusual, compared to all the schools Adam had ever seen. The incredible tropical flora was present everywhere. Monkey pod trees, Royal palm trees, yellow shower trees, hibiscus, ginger, and thousands of other plants were overtaking the grounds. The buildings were designed with the idea of creating shade. Hallways and walkways were all on the exterior, covered by overhangs and cantilevered sun devices. Everyone was wearing flip-flops, flowered shirts, and shorts. Adam was clearly overdressed in his suit and tie. Kelly seemed to have fun just watching Adam's expressions. He was trying to take it all in, process the overwhelming stream of information and the new environment. The School of Architecture was in an old building so deteriorated that the termites must have eaten every shred of its fiber twice. It was held by paint and a prayer. But it had its charm, and Kelly and Adam were told to wait for the dean to show up.

Finally the dean arrived. He was a man of few words. Rough around the edges, he gave Adam a few instructions, tips and warnings, as if the job carried some national security importance. It was hard to believe that he had been willing to go the extra mile to invite Adam in spite of the sea of red tape. Adam reminded himself that the University had an entire department for processing the visiting staff visas. Still he had to wonder if he was there because of destiny. Was destiny just a stubborn mindset and persistence, combined with a possibility of an outcome that fit someone's imagination? Or a random collision of paths, the haphazard result of unintended circumstances?

Philosophers and lunatics have tried to find the answers to this puzzle since the beginning of mankind. Looking back from the safety of old age, certain things make sense, as if they were the sun around which all the planets circulated. As if the accidental outcome was some logical means to determine the end result. Like a prescribed path and trajectory of planets. We'll never find out, Adam thought to himself.

Lecturing was second nature for Adam. After so many

discussions with his classmates and friends about the nature of art, his delivery was honed and confident. The material was charming too, so it went down very well. Art history and the architectural styles of Europe were a pleasant course, sort of a "Doric, Ionic, Corinthian" one, two, three. Another part of his job description was to lead a group of students in studio projects. In order to design architectural projects, one needs experience and inspiration. Adam's angle was one of a newcomer. He had a clear advantage of looking at things with fresh eyes and a different perspective.

The success of any design lies in the big idea. Call it a theme, or the character, but every project has to have the backbone of a good idea. Architects are often thinking about projects just like artists dream about new works of art. But the other, softer side of creation can't be forgotten. Adam found the sacred, inner space to motivate young students and help them lift the veil to see the future. Adam realized that teaching in Hawaii was a tour of beauty, an eternal presence in a promised land.

Soon, Adam found his groove. He discovered that swimming and surfing before work was healing. It was the most thrilling experience to paddle out to the sweet spot where the waves swelled up and carried the surfers towards the shore. The sun rose early in Hawaii, touching the moist leaves of persistent vegetation in Kapiolani Park under the motherly presence of Diamond Head as if the warmth was a reward for being faithful to the tropical god. The early sun created deep contrasts on the rock walls below the condominiums, while the sounds of the gentle morning waves created a background for the ritual of unloading the surfboards, attaching the leash to his ankle and jumping into the freshness of the blue waters. The morning sounds were different from any other part of the day. You could hear the crabs running across the sand with the receding waters. Adam listened to the sand, chattering as water seeped through it in relentless motion. And then, beyond the reef, the ocean swelled up like a beast breathing in and out.

The bigger waves came with a hum. The surfers made their decisive moves, aligning their bodies with the direction of the wave in a choreographed dance and paddle to catch speed. Soon, the wave was the dictator as the surf boards glided effortlessly down on the surface of the deep blue water, so cleansing, and so invigorating.

Adam had fallen in love with this ritual, the teasing game of approaching the reef and avoiding crashing into the sharp edges of the coral where the waves disintegrated into a white, foamy bubble bath. Once in a blue moon there was a morning when the ocean was calm as a sheet of glass. On those days Adam took out his paddle board, an ultra-light tongue of fiberglass made to glide on the smooth plane of water without much sound. The brown dolphins came up to play with incredible speed and joy. They approached straight on, as if they intended to crash into Adam, then in the last second they split and changed direction, enjoying this game over and over again. When the waters were calm like that, the ocean floor presented itself better than a Discovery Channel program. The fish were unafraid, even the ones that looked much like dinner. Adam observed the theatre around the reef, schools of glittering fish swimming in circles, luring him further and further out to the ocean. Suddenly, the ocean floor dropped and revealed the sheer cliff descending into the deep. Adam nearly panicked the first time his paddle board reached the edge of the abyss. The irony of floating on the water is that the brain thinks you will plummet down into the bottomless void. Yet nothing happens, and the board just keeps floating above the dark blue mass below.

Typically, after an hour of surfing, Adam finally caught the last wave all the way to the shore. He laid the board on the sand and stretched his tanned body on the warm beach under the coconut palms, looking at the leaves being tousled by the morning breeze. This spiritual rebirth, no matter how detailed in descriptions, has to be experienced for anyone to become a believer. As if the head got flushed out, the sinuses cleaned, and all the thoughts discarded. After a brief rest, the outdoor shower helped rinse off the sand, both from the surfboard and from the surfer, and the day began, fresh and new.

❧

The bigger picture felt even larger than anything Adam was used to. Teaching was going extremely well, both in the School of Architecture and at the Art Department, where he volunteered to assist a tenured professor with the art history classes. There was an empty art studio at the school, and it was offered to Adam rent-free. Now he could paint again, in the privacy of his solitude, accompanied only by geckos and an occasional cockroach. The breeze blew through the open window screen with rustling sounds, a secret language of leaves and vegetation.

Adam had enough cash to buy canvases, colorful

tubes of oil paint and turpentine, along with smooth brushes and linseed oil. Kelly and Jim did not see much of Adam anymore, so they made a point to meet at home for lunch when Kelly made her special tuna sandwiches. Adam felt a mixture of pride and nostalgia when he thought about his distance from home. He felt uneasy thinking about the oppression and the deceitful politics of the Communist party, how the party propaganda tried to smear and discredit the West. Rotten Capitalism, they used to call it. Very few people managed to grasp a full understanding of the impact of ideology on peoples' lives.

Manoa Valley was getting more and more foggy every morning. November brought showers and cooler temperatures. The old rock walls around Punahou High School were darker when the rain filled the porous stone. Down at the beach the sunrays touched the sand to warm it for the faithful. Often, the rain poured down inside the valley while the beaches happily basked in the sun. Adam stared at the magnificent colorful rainbows created by the sunrays meeting the moisture. Liquid sunshine is what the Kama-Aina locals called this phenomenon. The rain rarely lasted too long. Mauka showers were followed by the sunshine, which was the local weather reporter's mantra. The days went on just like they always did.

The new studio at the university was small, but it couldn't have felt better. Adam was so hungry for expressing his new ideas on canvas that soon after he started painting he produced several powerful works.

His entire life at this point felt like someone had opened a shaken can of soda. Once he felt the fresh air of newly attained freedom, he exploded with creative power. The new works were different from his art back in Czechoslovakia. The colors changed instantly, even though the subject matter remained similar. The titles indicated a new perception of color: *Red Rain*, *Yellow Nude*, and then *Crazy Kingdom* and *Falling through Time*. Within a month, he had finished ten new works. He was tapping into the stream of creativity that had been capped for so long. The works were all in his mind, ready to be placed on canvas. Adam spent a few nights in the studio, like in the days of Stevo's underground digs. In fact, he thought about Stevo often, and remembered how he once felt a need to present new work to his buddy and mentor, and how he had depended on Stevo's opinion.

The new painting, *Red Rain*, was inspired by the music of Peter Gabriel, and it depicted an abstract energy, very much like a lava flow at night. It looked like plasma radiating from a source of energy that was both infinite and inescapable. The hues of red color flowed in and out of each other, penetrating the viewer with a shamanic force. Adam mixed at least eight distinctively different reds. A deep blue background granted those highlights their supremacy and then let them loosely overflow and drip with the potency of a juicy pear. The image appeared very three dimensional. The work had a raw, urban feel, and was undeniably a baby of European expressionism. The vibrant colors throbbed with the pulse of Peter Gabriel's song.

Long nights at the studio were unquestionably a

tropical experience: energetic, yet balmy and peaceful. The nights were very yin and yang, like many other things in Hawaii. There was a sense of discovery and importance, even if this euphoria was subjective to Adam's search for himself. The third month into his new art eruption he was told about a group show, an exhibition of art created by the staff of the Art Department. He accepted the invitation and painted even more vigorously. Among many explosive paintings, some were painted hastily and impulsively, lacking a thorough intellectual process behind it. But other works were stunningly new, fresh and surprising, even to Adam.

Perhaps the process of creating expressionistic work is a trip into one's subconscious identity. Adam was exploring the impact of Hawaii and the New World on his state of mind. There was a radical development in what came out of him during his automatic painting experiments. Among the most surprising discoveries were the colors he used, changed by light and surroundings, reminding him of Gauguin in Tahiti. It was not all good, but not all bad either. Adam knew that things had to sit for a while, especially in art. He let it ferment on its own time, and came back to look at it later with fresh eyes. Then one day a new set of fresh eyes came into the studio attached to the body of Sonia Garcia.

Sonia was an Argentinean art dealer who happened to see an advertisement for the upcoming exhibition by the staff of the Art Department. She knew everyone on the list of participating artists except for one: Adam Keller. She made a mental note to see the new teacher's art. Real art dealers are curious, always looking, and Sonia was a work of art herself. She was slim and elegant with long black hair and eyes as deep as pieces of coal. She was a self confident woman, the type that did not take prisoners. When she came to Adam's art studio she wore a navy style dress and natural leather shoes with a sharp toe. Elegant to the core, she also brought a smile, and a light explanation of her intrusion, that sounded like an apology without being one. It was clear that the world was not offended that Sonia was leaving her footprints on it. She walked in and rearranged the world around to her liking. The world as Sonia perceived it was shaped like an amphitheater, with the center stage reserved for the eccentric woman with a radiant personality.

"I've heard about you, so I came to see what you're up to," explained Sonia after introducing herself.

"I am preparing some work for a show," Adam said.

"I know about that, and I am curious. What are you planning to show?"

"Well I can only show five pieces, and I have a few to choose from."

"Choosing seems to be an easy thing, but it never is," confirmed Sonia.

"That's pretty philosophical," commented Adam. "May be you can help me choose."

"I can help you," Sonia said confidently.

Adam showed her all the canvases, one by one, in the light of the photographic reflector hanging from the ceiling. They discussed sketches on paper, which Sonia loved, and then they reduced the choices to the actual pieces that would go in the show. It was down to eight but they needed to choose only five.

"OK, hombre. I got to go. But I like your work, and I want to offer you some level of representation. For the beginning, I just want to try how the market reacts to your work," Sonia said. Adam processed the conversation for a few seconds. Sonia seemed professional and knowledgeable.

"That's great!" said Adam after a short pause, "Next week I'll be done with the two canvases in progress, and I'd like your help choosing the final five."

Sonia thought she could do that and she left with her signature smile, her teeth on public display. Traces of her scent lingered in the air, but slowly the plumerias outside overpowered her fragrant perfume. The night came in through the open window and a gecko started to applaud with its rhythmic clapping sound. Adam settled down in his Salvation Army second-hand armchair and for a moment he was submerged in thoughts about the instant energy Sonia had brought into the room. Something about that navy blue dress wrapped around her cinnamon skin stayed in his memory.

Distance is a fuel for emotions, partly because people tend to have no arguments with those who aren't around. Human psychology can be very fragile in silence and solitude inflicting invisible wounds and provoking reactions unknown before.

Back in Czechoslovakia, people often lost the sense of identity. Under a mask of conformism used like a camouflage for survival, people pretended to agree with the principals and dogmas of communism, only to laugh at it in private, criticize it in the pubs, and do only what was necessary to keep their government jobs. Those who stood up were quickly eliminated, threatened, or punished. Even those who benefited from their association with the Communist party were basically pretenders, and in private they bought quality goods from the West like jeans and cosmetics, rock music and chocolate. In fact, the higher these individuals were on the ladder of the Marxist-Leninist propaganda machine, the better access they had to afford these "rotting" Capitalist products and many people even dressed in Western clothes, flaunting the latest fashions that made them feel special, sexy, and non-conformist. Adam was starting to recognize the impact of the controversial life he had escaped. An invisible change started to show in his mind, as if a huge wheel started to roll down the hill with nothing to stop its movement.

Surprisingly, Adam's first group show rendered some results. He went from being technically *unknown* to being *talked about*. The show was far more than just his participation in an event. His five canvases were carefully selected by the sexy Sonia Garcia before the final deadline. She came to his first studio at the university and spent hours discussing each painting and drawing to get to the core of his ideas, finding the right expression for the right impact. They selected five pieces that worked together and presented a body of work that brought something new to the general level of art in Honolulu. Sonia quickly had buyers for all but one of Adam's five works, but they had to wait till the opening reception so that Sonia could place the red dots on the wall next to his work. Sonia Garcia knew how to live. She also knew how to sell art and anything else, including some ice to Eskimos.

There is a profound connection between the environment and love, food and love, as well as music and love. These factors combined with relaxed times, result in triggers that create romantic relationships. It is an artificially induced sense of freedom in our perception of the moment, a temporary permission that our brain gives to the body in small doses of mysterious chemical components. Adam developed a very reliable ritual through which he could achieve those heights, and then paint all night in a trance, finding much of the outside world secondary and inconsequential. The gods honored the agreements and let him do this without paying a high price. Adam created almost a hundred works until there was no room to move anymore in his university art studio. It was time to find new digs.

Adam wanted a cheap space with a lot of ventilation. Someone mentioned Chinatown, a strange and transitional area at the border of Honolulu's downtown. Adam found himself walking amidst hundreds of Asian restaurants, produce stands at the Kekaulike Market, and gift shops owned by Vietnamese, Laotian, Thai, Korean, Chinese, Japanese, and Filipino vendors. Exotic vegetables were stacked in neat rows to entice buyers. The prices were low compared to supermarkets in other parts of town.

There was a long line in front of an inconspicuous restaurant with absolutely no design besides an exotic sign. Adam joined the waiting line and twenty minutes later he was sitting at a table covered with a pink table cloth. When the waiter came Adam pointed to the food at the table next to him, something that looked like a steaming tub of vegetables. When he finished the big bowl, his senses were entirely satisfied and his stomach full. Through the window of the Vietnamese place he observed the façade of a building across the street. Large double hung windows revealed an artist studio. Indeed, an artist was standing at an easel, painting. It was like a cheesy movie with predictable plot. But the art studio was there, right in front of him. Adam paid his bill and walked across the street to the building on the corner of King and River Streets. He discovered a hidden courtyard with banana trees, five cats, busy workers chopping and cleaning vegetables, and an open staircase to the upstairs lofts. The building was constructed entirely from lava rocks, a native masonry structure with timber floors. There were art studios everywhere.

A studio was available next to a Chinese painter who worked in a super realist style creating cityscapes and late night fast food diners with fluorescent lights and colorful countertops. Adam took a phone number for the manager and a week later he proudly moved his studio to the new location. It was entirely different from the academic feel of the university studios. This was exotic, open and inspiring. The drive was only fifteen minutes from his home in Manoa Valley and he was in his own world, transcending the convenient sensibilities of everyday life. Parking on River Street required parking karma, but his luck held. He noticed that every time he was looking for a parking spot, someone pulled out. Life was like a movie with a good script.

Adam started to paint larger works, as the new space allowed for sizeable canvases. His passion and inspiration moved in with him, like an old girlfriend. He believed that with every brush stroke he was closer to heaven. Suspended freely in the philosophy of expressionism when he worked, he discharged a little part of his anger that lingered deep inside his heart from the times back in Czechoslovakia. Canvases were coming to life in moments of epiphany and a state of bliss that came from a feeling of total freedom. He knew instinctively that he needed to find the means to enjoy that freedom. Feeling free and being free are two different issues. We can feel free even if in reality we are not being free. Being free, on the other hand, is a function of many factors that result in one's ability to simplify life to its essence of being.

Linen, paint and brushes were expensive, but Adam's combined income from teaching and art was good. His easel was a large wooden structure with vertical guides on which a horizontal support moved up or down, elevating the canvas to the right height. He stretched his canvas or linen over stretching bars made to size and the manual labor of preparing the blank canvas embodied a ritual, an artistic foreplay and a meditation before touching the white field with a wet brush. Adam felt a wild urge to express himself. He wanted to preserve an idea in its physicality, to use intellectual force to transform ephemeral thoughts into a tangible manifestation of the original impulse. Working on more than one canvas simultaneously helped to capture and clone a momentum, much like a freight train in motion. All the cars moved because one car moved. When he finished one work, the momentum caused the next work to unfold, reveal itself like a woman performing the dance of the seven veils. Like a survivor tending a fire that he had to keep burning.

❧

One evening after dinner in a fancy restaurant, Sonia came by the studio. She brought Adam a box of the heavenly meal she couldn't finish, and the taste of good wine on her breath. She brought half a bottle of Cabernet and a giggle, and she was hot. Adam stood up from his easel and came to greet her when she walked through the door. Her dark, long hair followed the curvature of her back. She put the bottle and the restaurant box on the cabinet and turned to Adam. "Hello," she said as they exchanged a light kiss, and her hand found the place where his shirt revealed his chest. There was a moment when she lingered, her chin up, reaching for another kiss.

This was a different kind of kiss, not just a social kiss. Her lips were slightly open and her eyes changed color. Adam was holding a brush in his right hand, but his left hand found the concave bend above her hips. Her mouth was hot, even compared to the tropical night outside. This time, their lips connected for a moment as he pinned her to the door, his body creasing her white linen dress. He felt her breasts on his chest, and she wrapped her leg around his body. She let his knee press between hers and he felt that Sonia was naked underneath her cocktail attire. She let his hand open the zipper on the back of her dress as she unbuttoned his shirt. Adam reached for the switch at the door and turned off the lights. It was a full moon and silver light

155

streamed through the opened window. Sonia's dress came off, and so did Adam's pants. They practically fell on the rattan sofa. The street below was still noisy. Sonia guided Adam to enter her. The sound of her orgasm blended with the loud Asian languages on the street below.

Sonia Garcia fell in love, first with Adam's art, then with Adam. She spent evenings assisting him in the studio, often sitting in the large sofa, sunken in a big cushion and reading without saying a word for hours. At other times, she read to Adam while he painted, grabbing material from art magazines and interesting books. She always took time to comment on his development and ask questions about his latest work in progress. Afterwards they found time to explore their bodies and express their physical love, which was both animal-like and beautiful. Sonia and Adam became friends, lovers and soul mates, although this change eroded the one-time simplicity of his life.

As a man, Adam found Sonia irresistible. After all she was an example of a raw Latin beauty. Besides her cinnamon skin, rich dark hair and sculpted lips, her high cheek bones and perfect legs, she radiated intellectual properties without being too bookish. Her wisdom was more on a cultural and social level, flavored with urban sophistication and experience. No man was able to resist. She could have been the mother of all sirens. Even beyond this, he was also completely smitten with her power as an art dealer and as a person who understood his art and had committed to represent him as he was.

Time was flowing like spring waters. It had been

more than a year since Adam arrived and the teaching gig was nearing its end. His exchange visa expired and the rules were clear. Visiting professors had to go back to the country of their origin and share their experiences for a minimum of two years before they could apply for a new visa. And so the dreadful moment finally came.

This was the last spasm of the Iron Curtain, but no one had a crystal ball. If Adam defected and simply stayed in Hawaii, there was no way to know what the consequences would be for his family back in Czechoslovakia. Adam thought about his father losing his job and struggling to keep afloat. Of the thousands who defected, many had regretted their decision because of the wrath it brought on their families from the Communist government. Indeed, this was part of the equation. The other part was Sonia. Adam could not explain his feelings. Typically, there was no logic to be found in the mystery of attraction. At first there was charm and temptation, then desire and permission, which only led to a new union of uncertain future. In the end Adam decided to comply with the visa regulations and pack his suitcases.

As if living a slow motion movie, the following weekends brought a garage sale, goodbye dinners with friends, and packing, sorting, discarding. Numerous friends believed they would not see him again and many tried to convince him to stay.

Sonia took all the artwork from Adam's studio, and only asked once if he would come back. He said he would, no doubt. Adam was extremely emotional about the untangling of his future there. He was leaving with part of his body resisting, kicking and screaming.

He had fallen in love with Hawaii and his painstakingly excavated freedom was to become a forgotten archaeological dig. Suspecting that the treasure lay only inches below, he felt a sense of an unfulfilled dream. He knew that he had only scratched the surface of his potential, and his return was like going back to prison. However hard and irrational, he was headed back to Bratislava. He arrived at the airport to find a Boeing 747 ready on the tarmac, promising nothing.

Slovakia, 1989

*I*nitially, everyone was happy. Initially, everyone was euphoric. People were taking to the streets in unison. The wheel of history was about to move. People were gathering in the squares and streets, surrounding podiums and stages and protecting speakers like Vaclav Havel. The talk of the town was freedom. Communism was suddenly dead. It took several months of excitement, discussions, and artful rendering of the future for people to understand what this meant. Adam participated in the crowds daily, bringing home news from the streets. The dissidents were finally winning. Freedom was in vogue again. Twenty years after the infamous Prague Spring and the Russian tanks, the esprit décor was openness and love. As though in a dream, love was palpable everywhere. It was truly a phenomenon, but this kind of euphoria happened several times in history. Everyone loved everyone. People held hands and sang in the streets. Connected minds. Harmony.

The Communists officially became the bad guys and people were ready to take action, but hatred and retribution were not very sound building blocks for a democratic future. Vaclav Havel knew that. He spent years in prison for political differences, and now he was the strongest link. He thought no one would benefit from arguments or fighting. The country could easily regress into a nationalist or political conflict. He started to promote mercy, clemency, and kindness. Adam was in awe, listening to Havel's brilliant speeches and seeing his actions. Much like Gandhi or Mother Theresa, Havel's role was historically defined.

Adam's father joined the crowd and marched to the Austrian border with metal shears. The crowd was clipping chunks of the chain link fences and cutting the miles of barbed wire. When the fences were all gone, people walked over the border back and forth ten times, getting the feel for freedom. They needed to make sure it was not just a dream. They needed to experience the moment of not being stopped and turned back.

In Berlin, the Wall crumbled. People attacked it with hammers and chisels, carrying away big chunks of it with them. Like ripping off meat from prey, the prize of being part of its collapse tasted sweet. Adam observed the ripple effect of unleashing human beings from their bondage.

People slowly created a new relationship with freedom. It looked like the romance of dating at first, then making love, and after a while, arguments and separations set in. Many former Communist countries dissolved in ethnic disagreements. Historic differences surfaced and hatred filled the vacuum after the dictatorships were gone. Bosnia, Serbia, the Baltic republics, and all other countries experienced some level of nationalism. Czechoslovakia was not spared. It was not the people as much as it was the politicians who wanted to separate the turfs in order to have full control over their territory. Corruption was the name of the game.

Adam though about Kirsten frequently during those days of liberation. What was she doing now? Adam digressed in his mind, wondering if she was still in Berlin. Now that he was in Europe and the Iron Curtain was gone, things surfaced. But they were just fleeting thoughts.

There was no letter from her in the pile of mail he came home to. And his heart was already compartmentalized into several sections. Art occupied a pretty large section, separated from the everyday by a tall wall. As if he needed to protect the most private of his passions, the most intimate inner expression of self.

Art was always sacred to Adam, something he shared only when he wanted to. Inside this compartment, there was a secret chamber where Sonia Garcia had a comfortable five-star suite. She lived within the art, or next to it. Adam was too busy to think about Sonia, but he did remember her every time he worked on his art. She was a part of his inspiration, whether it was conveniently self induced, or it latently dwelled in his mind. He discussed all his ideas with her. She analyzed his brush strokes. She was a part of the process. And he undeniably loved her as a woman, a seductress, and a muse. This love had invaded the space for art, and created a symbiosis, a realm where passion and convenience harmonized.

Slowly but surely, Adam's imposed home residency came to an end. It was clear that Czechoslovakia was experiencing slow start and a sputtering political takeover. Adam felt that his chances for success in art and design were left behind in America, and that his involuntary return had been a mistake. Now that his departure would not harm anyone, he was itching to get back. He was not sure what he wanted to happen, but it had to do with his psychic calling. Adam knew what he was drawn to, without knowing why. And not knowing why did not bother him. The question was how. He wanted to get back to America.

There was a state of chaos in Czechoslovakia, no one was in charge, and no limitations were in place. But he needed a working visa to go back to Hawaii. In a frenzy, he communicated with an architect he had met through the Brennans in Hawaii. Luckily, the architect thought a guy like Adam would be a great asset to his office. Petitions were filed, steps were taken, and again the Brennans were determined to help. As if destiny was showing Adam the door, the visa and all papers came in four months, a record time for approval of a working permit. Nothing could hold Adam back anymore. His mind was already in Honolulu.

Hawaii, 1991

The first artwork that came out of Adam's creative storage was a large, ten foot by six foot canvas depicting a street scene with a crowd of protesters rendered in a completely abstract, expressionistic way. He called it *In the Heat of the Revolution*, as it was based on his recent memories from the Velvet Revolution. He created it in an empty shed up on Tantalus, the mountain above Honolulu. Hidden amidst tropical vegetation, the termite palace was on its last leg. The structure was empty except for the giant mosquitoes that ate Adam alive while he painted. He couldn't stand it. His old art studio was not available, but another one opened up next door in the same building. He took it immediately.

Of course, the job with the architectural firm was waiting for him to validate his visa. He was now obligated to work there, much like a cooked lobster. As it turned out, the owner of the firm knew exactly how important the job was for Adam, and it turned out to be an arrangement for slavery. Pretty soon after his arrival, Adam found out that his pay would not cover half of the rent for a one bedroom apartment. His job description covered the design, drafting, consulting, the management of the office, and the marketing. He felt like his relationship to marketing was comparable to a drycleaner's relationship to the New York fashion week. He had no formal training in that field.

Adam's colleague in the Honolulu office was a nice Mormon architect with a large family to feed. He had more experience than Adam in certain things like construction documents, but he appreciated Adam's talent in design. In fact, they split up the work pretty much by preference, and Adam did all the design and the other guy did all the administrative work. As long as the boss was back in Seattle, everything was peaches. Still, the work was demanding with only two guys to handle so many projects. It took well over ten hours a day to get things done. Adam knew he couldn't quit this job while he waited for his papers. In order to survive in Hawaii, Adam had to resort to a second and third job. The second job was his art. The third income came from small interior design projects that weren't suitable for the firm he was working for.

Adam placed a medium sized drafting board in the corner of his living room where he worked on the small moonlighting projects. Money was tight but he made it work. Besides, it was what he agreed to. A green card in exchange for his work. There was no conversation about money, paycheck, working hours or other details, just a verbal agreement to work in the office. "You quit and you're packing your suitcases," said the boss. Adam had to start studying codes and regulations, rules of the architectural practice. All of it little by little. He decided that it would be a good idea to achieve some certification that would give him the authority to provide services worthy of his education. That permission was an architectural license, which was rather hard to get. Candidates had to take eleven tests, some of which consisted of three equally complex parts. Each test took more than two hours to complete and the tests were offered only once a year. Young architects generally only took a few of the tests each year. Adam took his chance and signed up for all of the tests at once. It was a three day marathon, test after test, and the results were announced three months later.

In spite of his Master's degree, Adam had to study all over again. At first, architecture seemed different in a foreign language. After he studied for several months, the new vocabulary finally started to sound familiar. He began to realize how similar everything was to the curriculum back in Czechoslovakia. He found the common language and passed all the tests but one his very first year. Nevertheless, it was a start. In three years, Adam became a licensed architect.

Then the Japanese stock market crashed. In the early '90s, Japanese investors and home owners were selling their homes in Hawaii for fifty cents on a dollar. The Japanese economy was so connected to real estate in Honolulu, that the problem in Japan soon became a Hawaiian problem. So many homes were sitting on the market at bargain prices that no one needed to build their own house. Builders and architects lost jobs. Adam did notice a decline in the revenues. He was marketing more and getting fewer projects. In a few months everything dried up. It was the first recession in Adam's professional life and his income dwindled even further. Money became tighter. It was necessary to ration groceries, count pennies, and work as many odd jobs as he could. On top of everything, his employer laid off Adam's associate and cut all the business expenses. Adam was left alone in the office and earned close to nothing. He wanted to quit. The boss reacted with sarcasm. "If you quit working for me, you're going back," he said. Going back was not the greatest option. Adam was living out his dream. The art studio in Chinatown was perfect, giving him a sense of freedom with his art. He was happy where he was.

Earning close to nothing from his slavery job at the sponsoring architectural firm, he relied on his art sales for extra income. Sonia Garcia was still keeping in touch, selling a piece here and there, although now she was busy with a new boyfriend. She still took Adam's breath away when she walked in the studio, but they both kept their clothes on. She analyzed his art work with a sharp wit, commenting on the colors and thematic trips she saw in it. Remarkably clear, she was able to describe the new in his work. She pointed out the direction and the development in each piece, and compared it to the national trends. Sonia emphasized how important it was to continue establishing his name and delivering quality pieces that mattered. Adam respected her observations and he also knew that if he made the first move, they would be back to the days of their erotic explorations and their late night discussions. But Adam knew that it was not desirable to create so much tension in his already chaotic life, so the former lovers kept their professional distance.

Adam had come to realize that life in Hawaii could turn into kitsch. Not that kitsch was always bad, but

Adam feared creative silence. Everything was too peaceful. He felt his artistic edge slipping away. His newly found fairytale existence was moving in a rut. He needed a jolt of energy, a nudge in his endeavors. He found out that the prominent artists in Hawaii were venturing outside the boundaries of the islands, and that they were exhibiting their work in front of the east coast audiences. His thoughts must have reached a universal consciousness, because shortly thereafter Sonia came unexpectedly to his art studio with a radiant smile and a brilliant idea. She was ready to take Adam's paintings to New York, presenting them at the Jacob Javits Convention Center on West 34th Street. She had just read about an International Art Fair where hundreds of galleries came to show their artists works.

She was curious to know if Adam was interested. There was nothing to think about. Art was his primary passion, and because architecture was not going so well in the depressed economic times, he decided very quickly. Sonia sold almost twenty works in one year, mostly to collectors in Hawaii. She knew it was time to introduce her artists in New York. She also knew several people from Buenos Aires who lived in New York. Some of them had connections in art and design circles, attracting wealth and class with a tango romance. She was determined to make it work.

"We are going to show in Nueva York, hombre," announced Sonia, in her typical manner, half joker and half enigma.

"How does it work?" Adam asked excitedly.

"We have to ship or bring paintings and drawings to New York, and install them a day before the opening

167

night. I'm taking three artists. You, Marcello Catellani, and Tim Bevan."

Adam knew the other two artists. They were very accomplished and seasoned artists from Buenos Aires. He was delighted to be in such company. He was opened to new adventures in part because he needed something new to happen on the art front. It couldn't have come at a better moment.

"I need help in New York," Sonia said suddenly. "Someone will have to help me handle the work, hang it and pack it, take care of the sales."

"You mean I should go with you?" Adam could hardly believe his luck. With a wink from Sonia it was set. He was going.

New York, 1992

New York greeted the couple with drizzly November weather. It was quite cold, particularly for those arriving from Hawaii. Adam and Sonia grabbed a taxi after they retrieved their luggage. The city was hectic, as if it was tirelessly proving its importance. It took almost an hour to get to Broadway where the cab spat them out in front of their hotel. A bed and breakfast in the middle of Manhattan was quite a find. The reservations were made months ahead, and they were told that it would have been impossible to get a room at the last minute.

Packing the artwork had been a tedious process. Each piece was wrapped in plastic, then in bubble wrap, and secured with clear tape. Individual pieces were separated with cardboard to make sure the corners wouldn't get scraped or the canvases dented. The artwork was carefully placed inside a strong plywood box built to size. Adam stuffed the remaining empty spaces with more bubble wrap before he tightened dozens of screws on the lid. Then there was the works on paper. Adam bought a piece of drain pipe from a hardware store. He even got two plastic lids, used for the same pipes as the end caps. It was indestructible. The bottom cap was glued on permanently and the top was screwed on with several predrilled screws. Duct tape was the last layer of protection for the rolled artwork inside. The packages were sent out several days ahead, arriving in New York the same day as Adam and Sonia. Timing was everything.

The hotel was not cheap so Adam agreed to share a room with Sonia. He had second thoughts about that after he agreed, but the other room was gone immediately. It was past midnight, so they just excavated their pajamas from the suitcases, took a quick shower and dove into the sheets. Each in their own bed, at first. Adam tried to keep some distance. Five minutes later, Sonia broke the rule. She slipped into Adam's bed decisively and pressed her hot body against his. She laughed freely, as if nothing else mattered.

"I want you," declared Sonia, leaving no doubt about what she had in mind. Rejecting her was not an option. It was also not in Adam's vocabulary. Their lips joined and the world immediately started to spin around. Her mouth was hot, as if she was running on high octane gasoline. He knew that mouth. His memories of hot nights in Chinatown were etched in his mind. Sonia was known to be unstoppable and she always got what she wanted. She stretched her body along his like a bow—the arrow pointing at her. She moaned and pushed herself closer.

"Adam, do what you want," she whispered to push his imagination. She rolled on top of him and played the active role. Moving in the rhythm of Argentine tango, she enjoyed calling the shots. At least this was the screenplay that ran through Adam's mind. So often, he had painted her in his pictures, sketching out her elastic body with Japanese inks, ebony crayons, soft pencils and pastels. While he sketched her image on the arch of acid free paper, she felt the pencil lines on her own body, as if gently tickling her skin in foreplay. Like a voodoo doll, she felt physical sensations at the touch of Adam's brush on the paper. By the time the picture was finished, she was ready for her prize. Adam did not resist, because resistance was punishable by Sonia's law. She reached easily for him.

It was early morning before they both fell asleep like babies. The dreams they had were dissimilar, distinctly apart and separated. They were not related to the erotic drama that just blasted through the room like a warm summer wind ruffling up the ocean of grass in the fields.

The morning came fast, too fast. But the business partners had to wake up, take a hot shower, and get going. This was the tough day of unpacking, installing the show, and making sure everything was working the way it was supposed to. Downstairs, the streets were busy. Cabs honking, buses with growling engines. People in New York dressed in black and walked with some convincingly important purpose. People of all races and colors chasing the one chance they were hoping for. Adam and Sonia hailed a cab.

The exhibition hall reminded Adam of an ant hill. Messy, and busy with a cacophony of conversations in dozens of languages and attitudes. Everyone was doing the same thing: tearing off wrappings, opening crates, and carefully handling the works of art. The fair organizers canvassed the floor, delivering labels, instructions, and restrictions. It was a total madhouse. Of course the art dealers got edgy under such pressure. It is just another game of survival, and in New York everyone was thinking big.

The crates littered the floor all around the booths and the corridors. This image was a strange landscape of its own. Some of the wooden boxes were eight feet tall with addresses, stamps, and other writings on them. The scale of the exhibition hall reminded Adam of some Egyptian construction site filled with slaves. The bizarre nature of the scene was underscored by the loud chatter in at least twenty different languages. The important dealers were certainly not there. Their slaves and worshippers were doing the preparations for the merrymaking. Their grand entrance was to be coordinated with the arrival of the collectors.

Sonia and Adam assumed parts of both the royalty and the slaves. Their roles were changing by the hour. First they had to prepare the show and decorate their raw space so that the illusion was complete. Everyone reached out for coffee, the legal drug of choice. One team had several huge cakes with yellow icing delivered to boost their moral. Pizza places made good money too. The final result was to be revealed the evening of the opening party. Lights were installed, wired, and plugged in. The power was turned on. And *voila*, the art sparkled. Everything looked like a gallery. Adam gave Sonia a kiss. They hugged and cheered. At three in the afternoon, the taxi took them back to the hotel. At around four, the organizers walked the floor to see that all the garbage and crates were removed from the stage. The vacuum cleaners sucked the last specs of dust from the runners in the hallways.

Adam stretched back on the bed. It had been quite a marathon. He was tired and wondered where Sonia got all her energy from. She seemed to be unstoppable. Her clothes came off practically on the run and they took turns in the shower. The hot water took some of the fatigue away. Sonia pulled a gorgeous dress from her suitcase. She coordinated her garment with jewelry, mostly black pearls. Adam was stunned by the perfect woman in front of him. She did her hair up in a hip and sassy manner, while holding the hair pins between her lips like a carpenter would hold a few finish nails. It was a quick transformation, yet the result was striking. She left her smooth bangs out to frame her face, and left some hair loose for a relaxed appearance. It was time to head back to the show.

～～

The limousines arrived, bringing special invitation guests. It was the preview show, for the VIP guests and the press. The New York art critics were the intellectual, self-indulgent, self-important kings and queens of the art world theater. Writing about the intangible. They affected the value of art in millions of dollars, transforming the ingenious yet elusive works of art into commodities. They describe the important trophies for the modern hunter-gatherer. All of them were arriving.

Standing at the booth in the art fair at first seemed glamorous. It fed the ego of the dealer and it certainly felt like success to the artist. During the VIP evening, pretty waitresses delivered drinks while walking around in short skirts with trays of food and slices of chocolate cake. Maybe some people came to this world all smart and ready, but Adam was not prepared for the big world. He was still blinded by the spotlight, and he forgot what stage he was on. Little by little, by no fault of anyone involved, he started to recognize the basics. It felt like a revelation. He realized that they were in an art fair that featured mostly commercial art, prints, and editions by famous celebrity artists exploited to the last drop by large publishing corporations. Many of the artists represented at the fair had no clue just how much they were juiced for profits, mostly because they were dead. Those who were still kicking were not really visual artists, they were actors and singers or rockers who, bored with concert tours, let their god syndrome go loose as they took some extra pills and started to paint.

Adam and Sonia took turns walking around the exhibits. Acres and acres of commercial works of art were presented in amazing frames, some of which cost more than the art. Suddenly Adam realized that they were in the wrong venue. He frantically walked around the exhibition hall, looking for some art he could respect and look up to. There were pockets of quality, but it was maybe only ten percent of all the art presented. He talked to the people in charge of those booths, conducting his own desperate research. Most of those dealers were at the fair for the first time and had not known what to expect. Adam thought hard about how to approach Sonia with this information. She was as sweet as ever, smiling at potential buyers while Adam was sliding deep down into an abyss of doubt and desperation. Like seeing an enormous pedestal with some ancient idol falling down, broken into thousands of pieces. He snapped out of this reverie when he realized that he was standing at the wall of the public relations booth, sweating. He had lost all sense of time, so he walked back to join Sonia. When he was approaching their booth, he noticed she was talking to a remarkably pretty blond and a very well dressed man with the art fair catalog in his hands. They were analyzing Adam's art on the walls, pointing and discussing it.

"That is a perfect choice, I can tell you," said Sonia.

"It's something we did not expect to find here at this fair—so new and raw," the man said.

"This is the artist," offered Sonia, turning around on her stilettos. "He's here in New York for the first time."

"We are in love with your artwork. We have just bought your two *Yoga* paintings," said the man.

Adam had painted a series of oils on linen from Belgium. The expressionistic figures in the paintings seemed to be performing yogic poses, but they were also naked. The male figures had erected penises and the women stretched in extreme positions.

"This is Mr. and Mrs. Jergens," Sonia introduced the couple, "and this is Adam Keller."

The Jergens went on and on about how they loved Adam's work until another man in black cut in.

"Don't mean to interrupt, but this is the best art in the entire fair. It is the only art with an edge in the whole place," said the man. "I'm surprised to find this here. How much is the blue nude?"

"Eight thousand," said Sonia, showing her teeth with

a wide smile as she managed her hair and voice.

"Is it oil?" inquired the man.

"Oil on linen," Sonia said. She returned to the couple who bought the two paintings from the yoga series. "Thank you for your purchase," she said. "You have a good eye, obviously. We'll stay in touch."

"We are going to enjoy these," Mr. Jergens said. "Nice meeting you, Mr. Keller." They left as the other guy in black bought the *Blue Nude*.

Like wiping the tears from a child's face, Adam retracted his negative thoughts about the fair and the uneven quality of art presented there. Just a story of a different and unique artist, perhaps temporarily in the wrong venue. But the fact that he was so different and non-commercial made his art stand out. During the course of the preview evening, a miracle happened—all his art sold, and Sonia wrote down names of collectors who wanted to see other works. The organizers tried not to let anyone walk out with the art because that meant that some booths would be empty and the show would be over. After Adam's last work was sold, he and Sonia sat down in the two armchairs provided by the fair and stared at each other in disbelief. There was a moment of silence, then Sonia started to giggle and Adam followed suit, until they both burst out in laughter, not knowing what hit them. It was quite unexpected, to sell sixteen works in two hours. All of a sudden, there was no panic. It was a very liberating feeling. The work was done and the rest was play.

Art is supposed to be the ultimate freedom of expressing ideas. Art can be anything you want, so how is it that there is the unique and special works of art, while at the same time there is another kind of work that has merely decorative value? If there is freedom in creating art, isn't it up to the artist to make whatever he or she pleases? Why is art being judged and categorized? Who is behind this ploy?

Obviously, artists need to make a living. The dealers and galleries want to make a living, and they do so, because there is a demand for art. There must be someone who makes all the calls. Adam thought about the freedom he felt when he was in his art studio. If he let himself be influenced by the demand for a specific expression, he would lose the sense of freedom and he would start to only produce things mechanically. Working for the market is the death of art, at least for the artist who is seeking the ultimate freedom. Artistic freedom is the right to disobey, the unwillingness to conform to society's artificial standards. Only the rebel is free. Purity of mind, uncluttered by what others may think of it. Art is rebellion. Art is resistance.

The dealers transform art into a commodity. Artistic works presented as products of pure and intrinsic beauty, yet traded for currency, starts the cycle of corruption. But what artist wouldn't want to be a star? Famous artists make a lot of money in a short time. Adam imagined having a lot of money. It was a very abstract concept, but clearly creating for the market with sales in mind made the art commercial. But what about Andy Warhol? Adam wondered. Warhol openly admitted he was creating art as a product in his factory. Acres of art.

Real artists did not think about money, or did they? Adam wasn't sure he knew the answer to that yet.

Adam thought that the world of art was immense, indescribable, and impossible to categorize. If he excluded all art that was created in pursuit of monetary gain, he would be reducing the art world to the honest, pure, and direct, like a good French sauce. But he wondered where the talent factor came in. Could there be a talented artist who became famous and was now making millions with his art? Or could there only be impostors, who, having employed an army of public relations experts, became merely a celebrity. Adam stopped his train of thoughts to stay away from the insanity.

The evening was nearing its end and the party was over. Sonia could not talk anymore, as her voice started to feel the fatigue. It was time to turn off the lights, call the cab and get some sleep. The hotel room was cozy and the hot shower felt invigorating. The adrenaline, pumping in Adam's veins, kept his mind going. They were still discussing the success of the evening. Success can taste sweet. For many, success is an aphrodisiac. The former, and now accidental, lovers brushed their teeth, and slipped into their pajamas.

Sonia loved a body lotion with a light fragrance so that she always smelled like someone stepping out of the shower. The lights were dim, and Adam came close to her at the bathroom vanity. She observed herself in the mirror as his arms surrounded her in a warm embrace. She liked her image in the mirror. His mouth covered her neck with hot breath and kisses. The feeling of his lips on her neck was just the edge, yet it connected with the animal inside her. She wanted more. Sonia turned her body around and found Adam's lips. He lifted her on the vanity counter and connected with her hot lips. He remembered the inner temperature of her mouth. She surrounded him with her legs and clamped tight. Adam carried her to the bed, pausing at a wall where she managed to open her bra and take off his tee shirt. Their lips were touching through all their acrobatics, and they made love, pure and undiluted.

"I love you," whispered Sonia when they emerged from their altered state. "I always will."

Adam was silent, because the question he had on his mind would spoil the moment. She caught his thought telepathically. "I know," she continued, "I did not think you would come back. I needed someone."

Adam kept silent. It did not matter. The fact that she had another man was irrelevant at the moment. It wouldn't change the outcome, and it didn't.

Adam just kept looking at her beautiful profile in the dim golden light spilling over from the alabaster wall sconces in the bathroom. Sonia was a gift from the gods. But she was a wild spirit, an untamed animal with unpredictable behavior. She knew who she was. She did not want to change. When she loved, she loved completely. Loving two men was within the acceptable limits of her liberal mind, but in passionate denial Adam thought that she really loved him more. May be all men would think alike in this situation. Like jumping in a wild river, once in the stream, there was never a right moment to stop and ask.

Thoughts of his family back home and the other people he had loved were sometimes painfully present, and yet sometimes he lived in a strange, parallel reality, void of any immediate feelings. His world was one of hard idealism, romantic only about art and everything that surrounded it. The art world became an obsession, much beyond a hobby, somewhat of an addiction. Adam did not know that, or maybe he was just in a denial about that too. The price was high; no one gets something for nothing. Knowing one's limitations can make freedom bittersweet.

The three days of the fair were satisfying because they reflected the success of the very first evening. As it was often the case, two or three works could sell ten times over. Occasionally, an artist made work so deep and balanced that the viewer was attracted to its lure, artistic or rational. Perhaps "artistic" is the true opposite of "rational." Yet the best works of art possess both qualities, as if they have to co-exist to satisfy the spirit.

Thousands of people passed by Sonia and Adam's booth and looked. Some asked questions and some got into analyzing the work on the walls. On the third day, a woman dressed in a Chanel suit with her red hair tied into a ponytail, returned to the booth to talk to Sonia. Adam stood off to the side and tried to appear as if he was busy with some paperwork.

"I am impressed by your artists, especially Keller," the woman said, initiating the conversation. "Sorry, I should introduce myself, I am Rachel Goldfarb, and I have a gallery here in New York."

"Which one?" Sonia asked. Her curiosity was peaked.

"*Gallery 505*. It's the street number of the first gallery I owned, and when we moved, I kept it."

"Of course, you are in Chelsea," Sonia said, brightening.

"Did you sell all this work here?" Rachel asked.

"Yes, we sold almost everything the very first evening."

"That is quite remarkable, in a fair that is more commercial in its makeup."

"We did not know what to expect, so we are pleasantly surprised," Sonia admitted rather honestly.

"Would you be open to letting me try Keller in New York? I saw the pieces you sold and the ones with the yoga theme are very good."

Sonia gulped, realizing the significance of Rachel's offer. *Gallery 505* was one of the heavyweights. In the infinite spaces of the art universe, Rachel's gallery was a supernova. Not only did their prime location in Chelsea secure exposure, but they had shown cutting edge art consistently for several years.

"It is a great honor to hear this from you, Rachel, and I think the answer is yes," Sonia said calmly. She was capable of hiding emotions, but Adam noticed the movement of her chest, suppressing her heartbeat.

The two women talked about the details. It became clear that this kind of gallery observed the artist for two years before they would decide to hang a show. Sonia would have to keep in touch while Adam painted new works, and they would have to send images on a regular basis. After a while, Rachel was ready to leave. Sonia saw Adam listening in, moving closer and closer, but she ignored him, much like ignoring a dog as it crawled closer and closer to the dinner table. She did not introduce Adam to Rachel, although she had introduced him to many visitors at the fair. Instead, she saw Rachel out, smiling. Adam wanted to discuss this, yet he had decided to wait. An unanswered question lingered in his mind.

Hawaii, 1991

The trip to New York was over, and things slipped back to the old groove in a hurry. The good news was the few thousand dollars that Adam brought back from the art fair. The bad news was the fact that things suddenly turned quiet, as if this crucial episode in the matters of art hadn't even happened. Somewhere, someone turned the faucet off. The silence after every storm. As soon as the suitcases were unpacked and the laundry washed, there was no evidence of the positive action that had taken place just a few days ago.

Like turning to a new chapter of the book, Sonia went back to her life with her new boyfriend, as if the trip to New York had been just a distant memory. Adam went back to his life too, frantically trying to catch up with all architectural projects he had neglected for a week. Everything appeared so promising in the moment, while they were tending the booth full of art in New York. All the art sales, inquiries, the talk.... Peoples' attention was released like a quick sexual act, concentrated within a few minutes of opportune social conversations, just a game of scoring points for being in the know. All the hoopla seemed forgotten, even before they left the fair.

Adam thought about the notion of providence a lot after he returned to Hawaii. He might have returned, but the paintings he had sold were now out in the world. He thought about the fate of the collection of art stolen from his grandfather. Those were carefully selected works, directly purchased from the artists, discussed, valued, and cherished by the entire family. Would these masterpieces ever surface? Would he even recognize them if they did?

Sonia kept visiting the quiet art studio, which felt more like a fireplace that went out in the evening, and was damp and cold in the morning. Of course Adam started to draw and paint again, but the jumpstart was somewhat difficult. His best method for getting back into his routine was to make a pot of good coffee, listen to familiar songs and daydream.

He thought often about his on-and-off relationship with Sonia. As Adam saw it, it was pretty much over. He knew that an aspect of the relationship was based on affection and that the friendship would stay intact. The hot romance hadn't fizzled out, but it had to stop, or it would erode his peace. Sonia finally got engaged to her new boyfriend, who was from Buenos Aires. He was from a very established family and she was looking at a good life with him, without worries and struggle. There were moments of regret in Adam's mind, wishing he would have never gotten into such a situation with her, but he reminded himself that there was no need to regret. It all boiled down to memories and marks on the soul no one could erase, experiences he would not be able to obliterate. But would he want to forget? If pushed back in time, would there have been a different outcome? Probably not, he thought ruefully.

Honolulu also never failed to deliver beauty and a sense of promise. Humidity, sunshine, and the warm climate suggested a perpetual rebirth, a possibility in the air. Each morning, all was new, and the cards were shuffled. The desire to live fully never left Adam's mind. It also presented itself in his works. With new ideas from New York, Adam painted vigorously, but his first work depicted an empty room with just one figure in a meditative position called *Blue Fire*. It was an oil painting. There were other works from that period, when he explored the perils of being in love with a femme fatal. The active creation of art was clearly his source of happiness, the invigorating elixir of joy.

The architectural work was ongoing, with decent results, but it was clear that a serious career in architecture was hardly possible in Honolulu. The cost of living in Hawaii prevented most people from developing high-end homes, let alone publishable projects. Adam knew that the clients were a match to the small firm's reach, and for the time being it was paying his rent. After each workday, he went home with the breeze tousling his hair through the open roof of the old BMW he had bought cheaply from the Brennans. After dinner each night, Adam drove to his art retreat in Chinatown. The studio was becoming more comfortable and his thoughts were revolving around a lingering question: when something feels like it found its groove, when does the groove become a rut? Exploring his own reasons for staying in Hawaii also eroded his peace. It became increasingly displeasing to live below his mental and spiritual potential. Something else was calling. Some higher aspirations were nagging and disturbing his sleep.

Sonia was a very loving, decent human being. Like many others, she was seeking her own happiness, and she found it through her decision to settle down back in Buenos Aires. It was time to pack her gallery and say aloha to Honolulu. When Sonia left, there was a void. Suddenly, several things changed. Confusion was replaced by routine. Excitement became anticipation. Adam found out that erasing this relationship did not simplify anything. There was another turn of events. After New York, Sonia surprised Adam with an unexpected request.

"Even though I'm going to close the gallery, I will be doing more private art dealing," she began, staring at him boldly. "I am putting together a group of artists I will represent globally."

"What do you mean, globally?" Adam asked.

"Well, I will have a contract to represent artists globally, *para todo el mundo.*"

Adam was caught by surprise and needed a minute to think. "That sounds like you want exclusive contract," he said finally.

"Yes, something like that. You are on top of my list."

"Wow, Sonia, I don't think you have enough contacts or experience to do that."

"What do you mean?" Sonia's voice gained a scratchy confrontational sound.

"I mean that you don't know what the world of art will do to you as a dealer."

"I know what it will do," said Sonia, sounding self assured. "The world will buy art from me."

Adam could tell she was getting irritated. Her lips

shaped into a tight straight line when she was ready for an argument. "I just think you should try it out before you can demand exclusivity," reasoned Adam. "You can't have it *para todo el mundo* just yet."

"I can have what I want," Sonia said angrily.

"You can't have everything."

"I will not listen to you telling me what I can or can't have!" At this point Sonia was steaming. The art studio walls were not insulated, so the neighbors always witnessed any commotion. This time they were witnessing a fight.

"Look, you are leaving and dropping everything," Adam replied with his own anger. "Who knows where you will end up and what you'll be doing. I need to continue with my art and life. Nothing's wrong with doing business long distance, but you don't need any contract from me. We'll see how it goes in Argentina and then we can talk."

"Well it's your choice," Sonia said coldly.

"It's not my choice. You are the one who's quitting."

"Bueno, I don't care anymore. You can sell your stupid pictures wherever you want." By this time Sonia was holding a thick book about American contemporary art. She smashed the book into a bunch of tubes of paint and ceramic jars with brushes arranged on a work table. Suddenly, everything was flying across the room. To make her point clear, she grabbed another object, but changed her mind and just dropped it on the wood floor.

Sonia made a dramatic exit outside as well. She was talking loudly in Spanish, words that no one understood. Anger clouded her mind and her reasoning. She had gone a little too far. Some other artists were standing in the hallway, curious about the screaming. Preposterous as it was, this was the end of a relationship. Adam knew it was not really about the art, nor was it about the exclusive representation. Sometimes things got confusing, and reasons were mixed up with purpose. Words were just thrown into the recipe like exotic spice. The whole argument was about being cut loose, like an underweight fish that was released back into the water.

Adam sank in his sofa and stared into the old white washed rock wall. Nothing could penetrate the silence around the art studios. Or maybe it was just silent in Adam's head. The moment of nothingness lingered in the room for some time. Slowly, he came back to reality and decided to leave. The studio was left empty to process this event, to question the ghosts of the argument, and to render a fair judgment in the absence of the culprits.

There was, too, the factor of serendipity. It seemed quite ironic that after the big fight with Sonia, Adam got a call from the director of *Gallery 505* in Chelsea. Adam actually realized at the very moment she called that his life would not be the same. It wasn't clear how he knew it, he just knew. Since Rachel Goldfarb had not met Adam at the art fair because of Sonia's interventions, Rachel had to go through a little detective work to get Adam's phone number. And there she was, an art dealer from New York calling a little known artist. Adam's heart was pounding with excitement as he answered Rachel's questions.

"Have you been painting lately?" Rachel asked

"Yes, I have, slowly but surely," Adam explained. He immediately regretted his propensity for saying dull sentences and using ill-fitting idioms. It was so easy to hate the words that had just come out of his mouth.

"What body of work do you have since the fair?"

"My focus was to regain momentum, after all that happened in New York," Adam answered truthfully. "I am searching again for what is important for me to express."

"Like what?"

"You know, diving deeper into the abyss of who I am, even though that sounds very existentialist."

"Well, can you send me some slides? I'm considering including you in a group show of three artists in my gallery."

The silence on the other end of the line was just a result of interrupted breathing.

"Hello?"

"Yes," Adam replied finally.

"I thought we lost the connection."

"No, no. I am just surprised by this kind of... unexpected news. Wow, I am very happy to hear this."

"I liked your work in New York, and I have all the slides Sonia gave me..."

"Sonia moved back to Buenos Aires."

"Oh. I didn't know that." Rachel paused, but only for a moment. "That's not a problem. We can work out details of the shipping and insurance."

Obviously Rachel was thinking in practical terms. Adam was always amazed by people who could operate in automatic gears. The costs of shipping, insurance, and the installation of a show that came from out of town could easily come to several thousand dollars.

"This is a great thing," Adam continued. "I will send you slides of my latest work. I don't have too many finished pieces since New York, but when I know that something is coming my excitement is off the charts and I paint a lot." It was the truth. Adam's inspiration was fueled by opportunities.

"I expect you are able to deliver your part. We will have a contract for the show. The schedule has to be kept, everything on time." Rachel sounded a little haughty and a bit arrogant. "I will wait for your slides and then I'll call you. Look for the contract we'll mail to you."

"Thank you so much for thinking of me."

"You are welcome. Good night," Rachel said, forgetting the time zone difference. It was still early afternoon in Hawaii.

Just to try it on like a new suit, Adam allowed himself to dream about New York and his mind went into overdrive. He imagined the streets of Manhattan, the brownstones and the windows of *Gallery 505*, with the halogen lights hitting the sweet spot of his new paintings. Never mind the daily grind at work, art meant more and more freedom. Something about the unraveling of new opportunities felt good. It gave Adam a feeling of achieving a new perspective, solely by showing his art. Every time a painting was finished Adam stared at it after he hung the new work on a nail central to the art studio's longest wall. Whatever it was, Adam wanted to explode, splash his emotions onto the raw canvas and attach his soul to the painting. His memory of the past, however perplexing, was still there, waiting to be harvested and repeated. He was searching, and boundaries had to be blown up. Limitations destroyed and people shocked. Art meant freedom, so the rules had to go. True freedom was resisting his current circumstances and pursuing what he discovered as his true self.

With the perspective of a show in New York, Adam attacked his art with a fervent energy. First, he rearranged his studio. He bought a new easel, much larger than the previous one. He bought a whole bunch of new CDs for inspiration. Music came to him as a natural companion, remedy for loneliness, sort of a fifteen dollars therapy. It worked every time.

Being hungry for a new beginning, Adam spent entire days in the studio, paying undivided attention to his work. The first piece was stunning. Six by six feet, a big square, it depicted two large faces, with a third figure swimming above them. The colors were deep, bright and daring. This piece set him on track to creating a whole series of works. Within three months he had ten new works, all large scale works painted on linen for quality. It was the most durable of surfaces, stretched, and primed with black gesso.

Soon, Adam finished several more works that put him on the map among the peers. Sometimes three or four artists got together for a break in one of the studios, boiled water for tea, and chatted about life. They got to critique the host artist's work. Adam loved that and everything else about the studio environment. It was a true community and it mattered to him. Rachel, the New York gallery owner, called at least once a month. She was on top of things; wanted a report on the progress. Not so much interested in the source of Adam's inspiration, she wanted to know how many new works she would be able to choose from, and how big those paintings were. "Send me new slides," was her mantra.

Naturally, Adam went to seek ideas deep inside. There he found a surefire place for finding the individual, unique expression of the sacred world. Painting is never just the surface of the paint, oil, turpentine, and varnish. It may not even be what the viewer sees. A true work of art is in the vibrations and the energy encoded in the action of painting, the same energy that behaves like a loaded gun or a time bomb, exploding at the right time in front of the right audience. The feelings expressed by an artist deriving from ultimate freedom stay naturally free, frozen in the moment. The power of a true work of art is locked up behind that surface, and the willing art lover needs a key, a code, and a combination within themselves in order to understand.

Adam worked as an architect during the day, but he kept painting every night. He came to work early, left at four thirty, and the studio was only a few blocks away. He painted till ten or so, because the show in New York was coming up soon. Saturdays and Sundays, Adam came to the studio at ten. Those were the best days, because he felt ultimately peaceful, like a frog in the wetlands. The streets were just waking up then, with tourists riding the Waikiki trolleys, the open vehicles with twenty or so tourists, making noises and screaming and laughing at the driver's jokes. Lunches were usually on the cheap, sometimes a Vietnamese pho, and other times a Panini sandwich with melted cheese on top.

Just around that time, a comedy show opened up in Honolulu, not far from Adam's studio. It was a dinner and a cabaret kind of show, but it was so good, it was sold out months in advance. Adam knew a producer, mostly from small talk while waiting in line for his daily dose of caffeine, who asked him to help design and paint props for the theater.

The actors were people from every corner of the world, products of circus schools in Russia, France, and Switzerland, magicians and jugglers, clowns and cabaret starlets. Those people lived on a different planet, sleeping during the day, waking up in the afternoon, reaching their climax in the evening when they delivered joyful performances to the "normal" people, who came to escape, forget, date, and gather gossip for the next day. The actors often gathered for an early dinner at the little Vietnamese restaurant on King Street, directly under the windows of Adam's art studio.

One of the artists Adam truly connected with was the magician known as the Maestro. His real name was Mikhail Beronin, a dark and enigmatic personality. They became instant friends based on a common belief that art was a rebellion and an escape from the "known" Universe. They clicked, and along with the magician's lovely contortionist wife, spent many great moments in Adam's studio on the nights when they did not perform. The Maestro was, indeed, very famous in LA, San Francisco, Paris and Germany, where he performed in many variety shows and productions. The depth of their minds connected them, the exploration of their memories. They had all survived communism, the common link of the East Bloc ex-patriots.

The crazy thing was that as Adam got to know the Maestro better, an unmistakable truth was surfacing: the guy was really a mysterious and supernatural being. He was not faking it, none of his actions that impacted people so radically were an act. He was the real deal. Sometimes frightening, as if he was the descendant of Rasputin, he was able to read his audience like a book. He visited their minds, browsed through their memories, and guessed their secrets. He made people do things. He had such a charisma, that women in particular imagined some mystical connection, feeling his energy somewhere between their legs. It was a truly strange phenomenon, the whole spiel. Nevertheless, Beronin was a good person with a heart of gold. He enjoyed being with other artists, sharing the intangible connection, the art of freedom. With Adam as his new friend, he found a sparring partner in the monkey business: two Huck Finns in one town.

What is life and where is it leading us? Adam and Beronin discussed the heaviest existentialist topics at parties, where wine and vodka were abundant. *Quo Vadis* was the next painting that Adam created from these conversations. Everyone had an infatuation with life as if they were in a state of a permanent love affair with the world. Adam's entire experience of being in the center of Bohemian life was, unmistakably, a déjà vu from the times of Stevo's underground studio. With a feeling of new beginnings, anything was possible and all was new again. Adam had flashbacks from his life in Czechoslovakia and many images popped up in his mind. Vividly present, old friends surfaced in the daydreams. Individual characters didn't matter as much as Stevo and his influence on the crowd. Adam's new artwork was born of the purity of this conscious wakefulness.

He was also getting closer and closer in his presentation to Rachel, his bid on his destiny. He hoped that New York would be there with him. New paintings were lined up along the walls of the studio, like birds on electric power lines. Looking at the new body of work, Adam felt a sense of completion, an energy field with a substantial, rock-hard quality. With Adam, it worked like this: the art piece showed up in his mind finished and final. Then it was just a matter of time to execute the image, and stay as close and truthful to the original saved in his mind. Adam's method was to meditate and visualize the whole show in advance. He was seen pacing nervously without many words for hours, becoming distant and focused. He forced his mind to go beyond the visible spectrum of things around him. Suddenly, he was not present in the reality around him. It was as if stepping out into the future, like fast-forwarding to the time of hanging his new show. A remote viewing of his own show. After achieving that experience, it was just a pleasant few months to prepare the new exhibition, piece by piece.

On a Tuesday morning around mid-May, Adam dialed New York. The galleries were typically closed to the public on Mondays. After the receptionist finished his screening routine, Rachel picked up and showered Adam with accolades. She had received Adam's slides and loved them.

"Your new work is better than I imagined. It has power."

"Thank you, Rachel. Which piece do you like best?"

"I don't have a favorite, although the one that speaks to me most is *Being*. Oh, and also *Mutation*."

"Thank you, both of them stand for all that I really want to say with my art. Why I actually paint."

"I can feel it. I decided I am going to show eleven of your new works. This will be a three artist show. You, Kevin Mackey, and Tracy Cohen. All three of you produce strong work, although very different."

"You know, Rachel, this show in New York means a whole lot to me. I was dreaming about this all my young years. I want to make it good."

"We'll see how it will be received, Adam. You never know until you put it in front of the viewer. They may fall in love or they may stay cold to your work. It depends on the constellation of many stars. We hope it is your lucky star."

"Thank you. I am already lucky to have someone like you giving me this opportunity. Many artists would kill for this to happen."

"Don't kill. Paint," Rachel said laughing.

"I will finish three works that are almost done. I hope they will dry fast, so that I can pack them and ship them. You will like these, they are about energy. The way I see energy now."

"Send the slides as soon as you can take photographs. I may have buyers sooner than the show will be up."

"Really?" Adam was surprised.

"I hope so. People trust my judgment when it comes to new art. I have not disappointed them too many times. Anyway, have to go. We'll talk soon."

"Okay. Thank you again."

Adam felt a strong meaning in the ease of communicating with Rachel. Inexplicable ease which replaced the impossibility of actually getting near a gallery owner of her caliber. The years of trying, failing, and receiving hundreds of rejections, were now in the haze of history. The invisible stone wall was gone. It seemed as if destiny had arrived to the shore. Once on dry land and no longer seasick, Adam saw no obstacles in his career. A fantasy magic wand at work, as if Beronin had sprinkled the sparkly dust on his life and changed it for good. He felt as if most of his good ideas came from the space between reality and imagination. To him it was definitely not from reality. The flash of freedom was delivered by the lucky moment of being in limbo, the gap in rational thinking. Freedom was pure meditation, a pendulum swinging between reality and truth.

Adam's architectural design work was still going on every day. Luckily, most of the clients were gracious, intelligent people who, after their construction job was finished, became good friends. Adam had a relatively busy social life that sometimes interfered with his work in the art studio. Shortly before the art work would be shipped to New York, Adam had to withdraw himself from much of his social commitments, becoming almost a recluse. Painting never felt like hard work, regardless how many nights he spent in the studio. Making art rarely resulted in exhaustion for Adam. Quite on the contrary, it seemed to have an invigorating and uplifting effect, somewhat hallucinatory, but that may have also been the fumes of turpentine, he thought with a smile.

Finally packing the work piece by piece was an exercise in patience and precision. The crates were large and heavy, and even with metal handles on their sides it was a serious Sisyphus ordeal. Each one carried four or five paintings, three crates altogether. And then they left, like children leaving for the world. They were finally shipped to find their destiny far away from the place they were born.

⁓

Weeks after shipping the work there was no sign of life or response from New York. Finally, one evening Rachel called again.

"Adam, everyone is excited," she said. "All my staff loves your work. It is very different, unusual in your thematic expression. I am happy with it, all of it. You know, you sold three pieces already, and we didn't even install the show yet."

"Wow, Rachel, that's great! But then we'll be short on my number of works."

"Don't worry," she said. "The sold works will be in the show with red dots next to them."

"When are you installing the show? I can help if you need me to."

"No, we don't need help. My staff does a great job. We install on Wednesday, the day before you arrive. Friday is the big day for you, the artists' reception. But make yourself available on Thursday night, for the VIP preview. Those are my sure collectors."

"My flight gets in at one in the afternoon. I'll get to the hotel, and I can be at the gallery by five quite comfortably."

"That sounds great. I need to introduce you to a bunch of people. The collectors always want to meet the artists. They are a hundred times more likely to buy someone's work if they meet the artist. Unless we have any more questions about the titles or the media, I will see you then. Be ready."

Adam's last two days before his flight to New York were consumed by shopping, mostly for clothes suitable for an art opening. Adam picked up the latest issues of all the art magazines after he was prompted by Rachel. The public relations consultant fired up many press releases, and the gallery got lucky: all the most important magazines listed the show on their calendar. It was a dream come true for Adam.

Now that all the artwork was shipped to its destination, Adam allowed himself to think about the past, his modest childhood, and the dear friends he had left behind. Did he do the right thing to leave everything behind? What about Kirsten? Adam quickly brushed away his philosophical digressions, because he knew the outcome of such emotional soul-searching. He was often saved from too much thinking by a simple urge to paint a new work. Liberated by the mechanical act of preparing a new canvas, shooting staples into the soft fir on the back of the stretching frame, and brushing the white gesso on the raw linen. His mind scrambled images of the works sent to New York, and compared them with a brand new image tickling the interior of his skull.

On the day before his flight Adam painted a fresh work, making him regret the trip. Much like a child refusing to retreat to the bedroom, he painted until the wee hours of the morning.

Deep down, he knew that the creative part in him did not need the show, the formal recognition and accounting. It was the ego that craved the fame and glory. Diving into the creative process saved many artists from the jump into the abyss of disappointment and resignation. As Sonia had warned him so long ago, he knew that the recognition only came at a price, and sometimes not at all. But still he knew he loved the process completely. As he put away his brushes and packed the final things in his suitcase, he knew he was ready for whatever would happen.

New York, 1993

October in New York offered the dazzling air of an Indian summer, warm rays of sunshine kissing the buildings at a low angle. The cab rushed Adam to the hotel where he unpacked, took a shower, and slipped into the New York art uniform of all black. The VIP opening started at five, promising everything and nothing. It was a seal of approval or death for the artist, much like the Roman Caesars giving their thumbs up or thumbs down. There was a mixture of curiosity and anxiety on Adam's mind, as much as he wanted to be nonchalant about it. If he worked all his conscious life towards a presentation, this was it. A gallery like this would show his work to the world of art collectors who recognized quality, novelty, and a uniqueness of style. It was all somewhat unpredictable and risky. The cab passed the Chelsea Hotel, with its balconies casting shadows on the old façade as the sun set somewhere west of the Hudson River.

The last of the daylight was fading rapidly. The gallery windows illuminated the street with the power of their halogen light bulbs. Inside, there was a crowd all clad in black, standing in groups and debating, strangely gesturing in some tribal dance movements. Many were looking at the art on the walls as Adam hurried towards the entrance. Outside, the world was holding onto its sanity, the relative peace and quiet of the street, with only a few honks from yellow cabs. Inside, the chatter amounted to a symphony of a beehive. Men with their hair gelled back, women with short hairdos, all in reference to the latest Vogue magazine ads. Adam spotted Rachel, who excused herself from a conversation.

"Adam, finally, you are here," she said in a loud, confident voice. She radiated energy. "You are quite popular and your art is stirring interest. How was the flight?" She did not wait for an answer. "Come and see, you already sold five works tonight."

Adam gasped for air, and opened his mouth to say something, but that was not necessary. Rachel had all the answers.

"Let me introduce you to your new collectors. Excuse us," she said to a couple standing in their way. She took Adam under her wing and flew around the room, introducing her new star. On her way to the next room, she grabbed another artist. "This is Kevin Mackey, my sculptor. Kevin, this is Adam Keller."

Now she had two artists, one on each side and she seemed to be levitating just above the concrete floor. People were pleased to meet the artists, and Rachel finally let go of their arms, releasing the fish back into the stream. They were standing in front of one of Adam's paintings. A group of young people were also in front of the painting, discussing the drawing qualities of a figure that was centrally positioned in the picture. The mysterious figure was floating towards what seemed to be the surface, as if coming up for air. The body could have been either a swimmer in a vast ocean, or the Son of God, just taken down from the cross. Drawn with a white chalk on a black gesso background, the powerful piece captivated the attention of the group.

The waitress brought champagne. The crowd grew in number as Adam talked with the guests. The evening of the VIP preview was extraordinary in its reception and sales. It was also pleasant to be in conversation with true art connoisseurs, who instantly recognized the unique power of the artists' work. Kevin Mackey, a New Yorker, had his following, and there were only a handful of people who were not familiar with his work. He presented ceramic sculptures with animal forms that almost morphed into a variety of robotic shapes. The idea was genetic mutation, a form of secession from the natural world into a high tech hell.

Adam felt that there was so much to process. People were standing in front of his work, analyzing the veiled messages as if they could find them. Two hours later, Rachel was beaming with joy. She was not only proud of the triumph from a business perspective, but she had also talked with several art critics who seemed to be genuinely curious and inquisitive. The verdict would be published the next day. But the biggest accomplishment seemed to be the response of the key players who embraced the new and challenging work. Rachel whispered to Adam what one of the critics had said about his work—that it never dipped into the iconic simplicity of many blue chip works on the market. Instead, it engaged on the psychological and story-provoking level, which presented a risk, a danger of being rejected as overly intellectual. Thinking is not everyone's favorite pastime, Rachel reminded Adam.

"Tomorrow will be your big night," said Rachel with a smile. "There may be five times as many people coming and going all night."

It was hard to imagine a more involving evening than the one they just witnessed, but Adam was already hungry for it. He woke up the next morning craving a coffee boost. Only a block away he found a café with a line of fifteen men and women waiting for the same drug. He picked up the New York Times, and examined the cultural section. His show was listed and there was a review of the show in the art critical column. It read: "Three artists explore the meaning beyond the obvious." Adam's heart was pounding before he even took a sip of the cappuccino. He skimmed the paragraphs and found his name twice. They loved the show and they were talking about him. He wanted to shake the newspaper in the air and shout with joy.

The crazy city had noticed Adam's art. He thought it was quite perplexing how much resistance he had come up against in his life. The little acclaim, the very few sales, the constant struggle, and now something had come along with the power of a freight train engine and turned things upside down. With a proverbial Slavic superstition, he hesitated to accept it graciously, as he was looking for the catch, the trade off and the payment for the lucky turn of events he had encountered.

The morning sun touched his face ever so gently, not too eager to deliver warmth. He took it as a reminder that it was okay to feel good and accept his praise. The cappuccino had elevated his mood as he walked back to the hotel. Adam was exhausted from the preview party and he tried to take it easy as the day flowed like molasses. He ate random snacks while walking around Central Park, and visited the museums. The city was relentless in its energy, feeding everyone's spiritual hunger. Adam felt it running through him.

Evening came quickly and Adam rushed back to his hotel room so he could change for the public opening. It all started to make sense: the exhibition, the public relations, the advertising, the critics, and the artist being present and available to meet the collectors. As Adam hurried out of the hotel a man at the front desk ran up to hand Adam a phone message on a piece of stationary. It was from the magician Beronin, who was acting in a variety show in the city. Adam knew his friend was in New York, but he had forgotten in the rush of the show. He had no time now to search for his friend, let alone leave a message at the theater. He shoved the message in his pocket. He would deal with it later.

The evening started almost exactly like the night before. The gallery was illuminated as if the life source was inside, the cosmic energy captured in a trap and controlled by the powerful art dealer wizard. Again, the crowd was ready to witness a new event, the latest happening, and someone's success or failure—whatever the soup du jour turned out to be. The feeling was almost identical to the day before, groups gathered in front of the gallery, discussing theories about everything and nothing, or simply kvetching about the latest gossip.

The other artist, Kevin Mackey was already there. Adam could see him inside through the front door. Rachel was holding another piece by Kevin, brought from the back room for a collector who was interested in buying it. Just as Adam was about to enter the gallery, a familiar voice halted his motion. It was Beronin, greeting him with a broad smile across his face.

"Adam," Beronin said with remarkable intensity. It was the way only the Maestro could say a name, just one name, and yet imbue the sound of it with the full story of Adam being there in New York, his whole life and the curiosity that had driven him there. Beronin walked as if he was not even touching the ground. He appeared to be gliding effortlessly above the sidewalk, wearing a full-length black leather coat with studs and rivets along the edges. He was a magician, after all, so it seemed appropriately mysterious.

"Beronin! What a surprise. I was worried I had missed you," Adam said.

"New York is very different, isn't it Adam?" Beronin said as if they were only picking up one of their endless conversations. "We had to change the whole show. The New Yorkers have a great sense of humor, but very different from Seattle or San Francisco." He paused for a moment. "Adam, are you happy?" he asked suddenly.

"Yes, I think so," Adam said. It was not entirely convincing, and Beronin watched him closely.

"Look at you. You have a show in New York. You always wanted that. Tell me, are you happy?" Beronin asked again. Beronin's face always expressed much more than the words conveyed. He was constantly smiling, though quietly, around his eyes, much like someone who knew more than they let on.

"Well, I want your opinion on my art, my friend. You have not seen any of this," Adam finally replied.

"Let's go and see." The magician opened the door for Adam.

They both looked around the room. Adam realized that he was seeing the show from a brand new perspective that night. As if he finally had time to take it all in—the installation, the lighting, the curatorial intent from a distance.

Beronin slowly turned around and said in his melodic Russian accent, "Very good." He took time to study the individual pieces. He seemed to be impressed, nodding to himself. After a while, he smiled again. "Seems like you understand much more about life now...." His voice drifted off.

Adam was still discovering the show for himself. It was a sudden realization of detachment, a distance he needed to see things as an observer.

"Let's go outside for a cigarette," Beronin said. They left the crowd and stepped outside. The twilight crept in and the light from the cigarette was intensified in the darkness. Beronin inhaled and his words came woven in smoke. "In each painting, I can see your entire life. That makes a true work of art. For me, it is like looking into a Venetian mirror. Somewhat distorted, and somewhat unclear. Yet when I look deeper, I can see what I want. And I know all along that what I see is an illusion." Beronin took a long drag and exhaled another cloud of smoke.

"This show is a new one for me. I tried to dig up some essential truth. I really think I got at least a glimpse of it. I may be finally grasping what freedom is all about." Adam felt himself getting carried away. "Let's go back inside," he suggested quickly.

"Freedom, Adam, is the ability to forgive yourself for being truly alive, for living an inevitably messy life at full speed and making mistakes on the way." Beronin raised his eyebrows as he tried to speak through the noise of the crowd. "Life is messy. And everyone's truth is different, colorful like garbage in the ocean. Truth is just an agreement, anyway."

Adam looked across the room. Suddenly the world came to a stop. An elegant young woman stood there, hesitant, as if she was looking for someone in the crowd. Adam forgot to close his mouth, and stood there in a shock.

"Kirsten," he whispered. At that moment, the young woman finally found him in the crowd. He saw her lips say his name. Neither of them could move, and neither of them heard anything else around them. As if the world was set on mute and put in slow motion. What memories flashed through Adam's mind in that instant? In a split second he was back in Berlin, when her body disappeared in the dark of the night. Finally, he walked towards her. They stood in front of each other for what seemed an eternity, just staring at the impossibility of their appearance.

"How did you..." Adam found he could not finish his sentence.

"I read about your show. I had to come."

Their world changed color and hit a reset button as Kirsten started to explain her story. The two long lost friends and lovers entered into uncharted territory. And when they exhausted all that needed to be said, there was silence. Silence and forgiveness.

*M*ilan Heger was born in Czechoslovakia during the Cold War era. His ambitions to explore far away places had to be put on hold until 1991, when Milan and his family moved to Hawaii where he began to fulfill his dream of living in the free world.

Milan's life revolves around art and design. He writes regularly about art and architecture, contributing to national magazines and blogs. After moving to Seattle, he founded his firm Heger Architects, designing homes and furniture. His art is represented by Patricia Cameron Gallery.

Milan loves to spend his free time in the amazing outdoors of the Pacific North West. He is an avid tennis player and a bike rider.

Acknowledgements

In the light of who I am, I thank my family for providing the environment of support and understanding for my writing. My gratitude goes to my wife Tamara, and children Livia and Robert. They are my source of inspiration.

I also thank my publisher Kristen Morris, editor Amelia Boldaji and Steve Montiglio for the great book design.

I am grateful to my friends who believe in me as a writer. To mention just a few, Patricia Cameron who shows my art internationally (Patricia Cameron Gallery, Seattle), Jane and Steve McGehee for seeing my book through the eyes of a cinematographer, Karan Dannenberg for her support and suggestions, Larry Heeren, Marsha Kabakov, and Paul Zievers who read the manuscript and many other friends whom I cherish and who cheered me on.

Milan Heger

Paintings

Like a UFO
Romulo

Missed the A Train

Flowers for Her

The Impossible Downward Spiral

Disposal of Virtual Experience

Artists Unite

~•~

Where I Belong

Origins of Passion

The Kiss

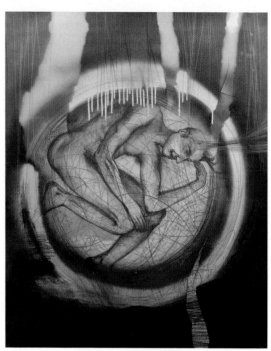

Return of the Rolling Man

All is Possible